She was staked out on the sun-baked ground

Dagger knelt beside her. In his right hand he held a tarantula by its back. He brought the hairy orange-and-black spider to within a foot of her face.

The terrorist tugged wildly against her bindings. Dagger dangled the spider six inches above her mouth. Its legs thrashed in the air.

"Don't let it touch me!" she screamed.

One of the hairy legs brushed her lips.

He didn't want to, but he had to; he had no other choice. Dagger grabbed her jaw and squeezed, forcing her mouth open.

Then he lowered the wriggling creature halfway into her open mouth.

"You tell me everything now, or I'll make you swallow this spider alive!"

Bystander killed in kidnap shooting

By E.R. Kern

ROME (Special)—As tourists and passersby cowered in terror, an elderly Roman businessman was snatched off a downtown street and a young woman, trying to protect a curious child, was shot and fatally wounded by the kidnappers.

The businessman, Emilio Boccanegra, was hustled away by two men and a woman on the Via Nazionale near the Piazza della Repubblica. A small child, apparently excited by the activity, wrestled out of its mother's protective grasp and ran toward the getaway car. One of the gunmen, apparently unaware of what was happening, seemed to panic and fired his handgun.

The young woman, later identified as Cara Francesca Carlson, ran into the street to bring the child back to its mother's protective side. She was struck by a stray bullet and died en route to the hospital.

No immediate demands were received from the kidnappers.

Police are following up on trying to identify the getaway car, though it was presumed to be a stolen vehicle.

DAGGER

THE
CENTAUR CONSPIRACY

CARL STEVENS

A GOLD EAGLE BOOK FROM
W*RLDWIDE

TORONTO • NEW YORK • LONDON • PARIS
AMSTERDAM • STOCKHOLM • HAMBURG
ATHENS • MILAN • TOKYO • SYDNEY

First edition September 1983

ISBN 0-373-61501-9

Special thanks and acknowledgment to Ray Obstfeld
for his contributions to this work.

Printed in Canada

1

"Ready to fly like the bird, *señor*?"

Christian Tulsa Daguerre poked and prodded each harness strap and buckle before answering. "As long as I don't drop like the stone."

"*Señor?*"

"Yeah, I'm ready."

"Then smile, *señor*," the teenager grinned, adjusting his blue Dodgers cap as he walked across the beach toward the waiting boat. "This will be fun. You will see."

"Fun, right," Daguerre muttered, still yanking on straps, testing buckles.

Someone from the small crowd of sunburned tourists wreathing him shouted, "Give 'em hell, pal," and raised his Bloody Mary to toast Daguerre. The ice cubes clinking and his own heart thumping were the only sounds Daguerre heard as he checked the same strap for the eighth time. Sand was sticking to his sweaty toes.

"Cute buns," a sexy feminine voice from the crowd drawled with a connoisseur's authority.

But as Daguerre twisted around to get a look at his admirer, the motorboat growled nastily and he was yanked off his feet into the air.

The red-and-yellow parachute bloomed above Daguerre's head like some giant tropical orchid. With each puff of the stiff sea breeze he felt the nylon shroud lines tug at the harness straps under his arms and between his legs, lifting him higher and higher into the pale Mexican sky.

And higher still.

"Let's go back for my stomach," he shouted at the motorboat, but they were too far below to hear anything.

Daguerre let go of the shroud lines with his right hand and tugged his drooping trunks back up to his waist. He wore only a black Casio diver's watch and these too-large swimming trunks he had hastily purchased that morning at Los Angeles International Airport as he ran to meet his plane. He grinned at the memory. It seemed there was always *one* thing he forgot to pack when traveling on assignment. Last time it had been his razor, the time before that his socks. He'd had to hop off the plane and immediately interview Prime Minister Thatcher with his hairy ankles peering out from under the cuffs of his three-piece suit. She had found it terribly amusing.

When the parachute finally stopped climbing the sky, Daguerre looked down, along his long lean body, across the flat stomach muscles ridged like a xylophone, past the occasional bullet, knife and miscellaneous scars that had fascinated Cara so. And over the edge of his sandy bare feet.

He stared at the 200-foot drop to the tiny beach below.

"Fun," he reminded himself aloud as he looked at the crawly insects down there that were once people. It was more crowded than he had realized when he first walked onto the beach a few minutes ago. But then Mazatlán always was this time of year. The gaudy hotels with their Olympic-sized pools only a short jog from the warm ocean reminded him of Miami and the time when he had sneaked Cara past the Secret Service guards to shake hands with the vice-president, whose campaign Daguerre had covered. Charmed by her wit and delighted by her beauty, the veep had been reluctant for them to go, despite the pesky aide who kept clearing his throat and waving a TWA schedule, and the embarrassed Secret Service man who glared hostilely at Daguerre. When they finally did leave, the politician gave Daguerre an envious wink, making him promise to bring her back again.

But that was last year, and Cara had been dead for quite some time now. Even suspended 200 feet above a Mexican beach, Daguerre knew exactly how much time. To the minute. He didn't even try to forget. Some things should never be forgotten, he thought, or forgiven.

A sudden gust bumped his parachute, lifted it a few feet, then moved on. He reached down again and pulled his drifting trunks higher on his waist.

"Another gust like that and everyone down there's going to know just how cute my buns really are," he said, then laughed for the first time in months. Surprisingly, this really was fun after all. And fun had been the one element missing from his life for too long now. Since Cara. His friends had tried to help with invitations and introductions, but soon realized there wasn't anything they could do. Daguerre's outward charm and openness masked a very private man. One who would heal his own wounds. In his own time, in his own way.

And this trip was supposed to be a start. Fun and sun. Sand and surf. Women and wine. All expenses paid and all he had to do was write a simple puff piece that any cherry journalist from Cornstalk, Iowa could handle.

It should have been simple.

But for some reason he kept feeling that familiar tingling at the nape of his neck that warned him something was wrong. A nagging tug of apprehension. Reporter's instinct, he called it, or soldier's sense. He had needed both just to stay alive this long.

He squinted down at the tiny paint-chipped motorboat that skipped over the mild ocean crests as it pulled him through the sky.

"That's odd," he said to the wind. "There are *three* men in that boat."

Yet when they'd strapped him into this harness a few minutes ago there had been only two, Fernando and Jesus. Cousins. Both barely eighteen. In the few minutes it had taken them to convince Daguerre to try the ride, they'd told him more about themselves than they had ever told any tourist before. Daguerre had that kind of face, that kind of sincerity. Jesus had only recently returned to Mazatlán after an unsuccessful attempt at crossing the border and was now working with Fernando to earn enough money to pay a reliable coyote next time. Fernando was already married and a father, eager to show Daguerre ocean-stained photos of his twin baby girls.

So who was the third man?

Daguerre shrugged against the straps, dismissing the extra man as just another cousin along for the ride. "He must have hopped in while I was fussing with these straps,'' Daguerre reasoned. Nothing to worry about.

But instinctively his muscles tightened. A cold wave of adrenaline splashed through his stomach. His eyebrows knotted. This was his reporter's response to any unanswered question.

He took a deep breath of salty air and tried to ignore it. After all, what could be wrong? Parasailing was a safe, popular tourist ride. Nothing sinister. For five American dollars you got towed about while drifting 200 feet above the ocean, the beach. The world. From up here everything looked simple, happy and peaceful. A pastoral painting by Andrew Wyeth. Now Daguerre could understand the attraction of such a ride to the typical tourist anxious for a relatively safe taste of adventure. Willing to risk a lifelong fear of heights for just a few minutes all alone. Above it all.

For Daguerre it was the first time he'd been able to enjoy the sensation of parachuting for its own sake, even though he'd jumped several times before. In Vietnam, covering the war from the frontline trenches, against the orders of both the military and his own bureau chief. Twice they'd thrown him out of the country, only to see him pop up again in the heart of a firefight, scribbling on a blood-spattered notebook. The soldiers respected him because he told the truth about what he saw, no matter who it offended. Even if he had to risk his own life to tell it. That respect got him into places no other reporter could go, *would* go, even if they could. He had been the same later in Iran, Lebanon, El Salvador, Afghanistan. Because of this, the other correspondents respectfully, and jealously, tagged him the Dagger, sharp and to the point. Willing to slice through the bone and gristle to get to the heart of a story. No matter whose heart he had to cut, some said.

The last time he'd parachuted had been at night, just north of the DMZ. A sympathetic sergeant had sneaked him aboard disguised as a medic. Daguerre hadn't bothered mentioning that that was only his third jump, nor that he was not overly fond of heights. The only thing on his mind that night had been to avoid getting hung up in the trees where snipers could easily finish him off. To land in a soft tuck-and-roll so as not to snap an ankle. To drag the chute and bury it. And to get the story.

Yes, he grinned now as the warm tropical breeze washed over his face, there hadn't been much time then to appreciate the view.

But today he was playing tourist. The call had come in unexpectedly to his Los Angeles answering service from an editor friend at *West Coast* magazine. They wanted Daguerre to write their annual Mexico travel piece as a reward for his exclusive interview with a group of Cuban mercenaries training in the Florida Everglades. Daguerre had protested that he didn't do those kind of stories anymore.

"C'mon, Dagger," his friend had argued when he returned the call. "You too good for this now? Not enough danger? Your hotel gotta have a land mine on your toilet seat before you'll go?"

"Give me a break, Danny. It's just that I haven't done this kind of fluff in years."

"We'll both make out on this deal, Dagger. You need the R & R and we pick up any *reasonable* expenses. Besides, if you don't go they'll send that bastard Clemmer.

And I hate the idea of him walking around the office with a better tan than mine."

Well, at least this article would be easier to research than the last. For that one Daguerre had trained along with those Cuban mercs in the swamp for two mosquito-infested weeks. Firing Uzis. Lobbing M-26 grenades. Listening to them rant about what they would do to Castro. But now all he had to do was pretend he was a first-time-to-Mexico tourist and do everything a tourist might. He even avoided speaking his near-fluent Spanish, relying instead on his English, German, French, Italian and occasionally, Russian, just to see what the reaction was. But local reaction depended less on language than on currency. In that regard, the deutsche mark was the most welcome.

"Paradise," Daguerre said as he hung suspended above the world, momentarily beyond his own past.

He looked up. Above him the chute fluttered and snapped, pregnant with wind, its cheerful bright colors stark against a pale blue sky.

He looked down. People roamed about the beach, splashed in the surf, bargained with the beach vendors over handmade puppets and sombreros. Sipped exotic drinks. Held hands. Kissed.

"Paradise," he nodded again when a spear of light from below stabbed his eye and made him glance back down at the motorboat. *"Damn!"*

This time it was more than a bad feeling. Something really was wrong. Terribly wrong.

The third man was standing in the boat, walking unsteadily toward the taut rope that stretched from the stern of the boat all the way up to Daguerre's har-

ness. Something in his hand flashed again in the sun.
A knife!

Daguerre's hands tightened into white fists around
the risers. He could see one of the other men in the boat
leap at the armed man. He recognized Fernando's blue
Dodgers cap. The knife flickered and suddenly young
Fernando was clutching his throat with both hands, trying to scream through the bubbling blood.

The man with the knife booted Fernando overboard,
then threatened the pilot, Jesus, who nodded with fright
and remained frozen behind the wheel. The killer shad-
ed his eyes with his free hand and stared up at Daguerre.
He might have been smiling beneath that thick black
mustache, or maybe just squinting. Daguerre couldn't
tell. But he could tell what was coming next. He gripped
the risers tighter in anticipation.

The man with the knife bent over the rope and began
sawing.

Daguerre felt the rope vibrate, then slacken. With
each new gust against the chute there was more give in
the rope. Below him was the crowded beach, the hotels,
the concrete wall separating one from the other. If he
dropped straight down he could hit the wall, the cars,
the hotel. People. Every object below was a potential
weapon aimed at him.

Suddenly the rope snapped free from the boat, wriggling upward like an attacking snake. The recoil jerked
Daguerre a few feet higher into the cloudless sky.

Then he began to drop. Toward the concrete wall and
the screaming crowd.

2

Everyone was moving.

Down on the beach people were frantically scattering outward like large ripples fleeing a freshly dropped rock. Cries of fear, horror and confusion spun upward until they assaulted Daguerre's ears.

The motorboat that had towed Daguerre was also moving, hugging the shoreline as it roared away from the pointing witnesses. Seconds after his rope had been cut, Daguerre had caught a glimpse of the mustached man as he'd thrust his bloody knife into young Jesus's back again and again, like a frustrated man chipping away at a stubborn block of ice. Afterward he shoved the bloody corpse overboard. The boat had then swerved around a bend and out of Daguerre's sight, cutting a white frothy scar through the placid green water.

But Daguerre had other things to concentrate on now. For he, also, was moving.

Downward.

The strong ocean breeze had pulled him back over the shore and he was dropping toward the hard earth with all its sharp, blunt, angular, cement, metallic and fleshy objects. Any one of which could cripple or kill him.

Daguerre's heart thudded against his chest like a boxer's speed bag, but he assessed the situation as he always did any danger—quickly and calmly. One thing he had learned from his father was that there was always more time in an emergency than the panicking mind realized. Take that time, his father had warned, use it to win. And Daguerre liked to win. Whether it was a basketball game in high school or an exclusive story for a paper, the thrill had always been in the winning. Forcing his will to dominate chance. Already his hands reached for the toggles attached to the parachute's rigging lines and he began to steer. Away from the beach. Toward the ocean.

He studied the chute as it fell. It wasn't the usual military surplus kind that you often found in Mexico; it was a fairly new sports chute with a nylon canopy. This type usually allowed a good forward speed of about twelve miles per hour. And much more maneuverability.

To the murmuring crowd below it looked like the greatest stroke of luck that the parachute was now drifting out over the ocean and away from the perils of land. But the few among the crowd who had skydiving experience knew better. They could tell by the way he worked the toggles and positioned his body that this was no amateur. Not a man who needed favors from Lady Luck.

Daguerre saw the ocean surface rising to meet him. Forty feet. Thirty. Twenty. Ten. His knees bent slightly in anticipation. His eyes were fixed on the horizon to prevent broken bones. His pale feet, not yet out in the sun long enough to renew his usual deep tan, seemed to hover over the placid green water a few seconds before finally plunging in. The water was surprisingly warm, like sweat.

Then the shock of landing.

He hadn't expected the water to be quite this shallow more than a hundred feet from shore. But it was. The salt water had barely lapped his chest when his feet struck the firm sand, compressed by billions of gallons of water. He felt the jolt rattle up his spine like a steam locomotive, but he was already shifting his body weight to absorb the shock.

Then it was over. He was safe.

The nylon canopy collapsed around him like a deflated balloon. Daguerre shrugged out of the harness, pulled the canopy from over his head and let the current drag it out to sea. He paused a moment to look where the motorboat had last been—and the two men who'd been stabbed. But he saw nothing. Neither the boat nor the teenagers' bodies.

Leaving the parachute floating behind him like a red-and-yellow oil spill, Daguerre swam toward the shore. The water was shallow enough to walk, but swimming was easier—and faster. And he was suddenly in a big hurry.

Several people from shore began to wade out into the water to offer help and ask questions.

"Are you all right, partner?" drawled a stocky man in a straw cowboy hat, a drink with a tiny paper umbrella floating in it clutched in one hand.

"Fine, thanks," Daguerre answered. "I'm fine."

"Well, that's fine, son. But just in case you want to sue the bastards, I'll be—"

"*Was ist loss?*" a gray-haired German in wire-rimmed glasses asked. "*Sind Sie gesund?*"

"*Ja, danke,*" Daguerre replied. "*Alles ist gut.*"

A shapely blond girl of about twenty, wearing a string bikini that strained hopelessly under the abundant curves, threw a beach towel around Daguerre's shoulders as he walked out of the water. He blotted his face, smiled at her and returned the towel.

"You can give it to me later." She smiled. "I'm in Room 208." She pointed at the hotel behind them, Hotel Playa Mazatlán. It was where many of the American tour groups stayed.

"I'll remember," Daguerre said, but waited for her to take the towel back. She did so with a pout.

Realizing that the danger was now over, other people began crowding around him, reaching for him, anxious to touch a survivor of a real catastrophe, as if some of his luck might rub off on them. They buzzed with questions.

"What the hell happened out there, man?"

"Mira, Cabron—¡Que bueno la tienes!"

"Hey, Jim, did you see what happened to those guys on the boat?"

"What boat?" Jim asked.

"I warned you about those parachute things, Harold," a middle-aged woman clucked at her husband. "I told you they weren't safe." Harold nodded agreement.

"Cut one sucker's throat, I'm telling you. I saw the blood spray. Shit."

"Stuck the other dude right in the back, man. Like Tony Perkins in *Psycho*."

But Daguerre wasn't listening. He nodded politely or smiled charmingly as they encircled him, but he never stood still. He shouldered his way through the crowd with a nudge here, a hip there and an occasional light shove. Soon he was free of them and racing across the Hotel Playa Mazatlán parking lot, his naked feet slapping on the sizzling pavement.

Fortunately, he never carried his wallet to the beach. Instead he kept a little cash and a Visa card tucked in the back pocket of his swimming trunks. Just enough to eat, drink and tip.

His feet were burning. When he'd come to the beach that morning he'd worn sandals, a terry-cloth jacket and sunglasses. But he didn't bother picking them up on his way out right now. He was anxious to get away from the cloying crowd—and possibly the police. He didn't want to answer their questions yet, especially since he didn't have any answers. Right now he just wanted to get back to his hotel and figure out why someone had just murdered two boys and tried to kill him.

And what he was going to do about it.

3

Daguerre crossed the Avenida del Mar the way he always crossed streets: against the light and against the traffic, dodging cars and insults with the same loose grin and casual shrug. Other pedestrians trying to follow him were usually sent scurrying back to the safety of the curb by two tons of racing automobile nipping at their butts. To the regret of those who tried to emulate him, Daguerre made everything look easier than it was.

It took no more than a nod to hail a *pulmonias*, one of the little white golf-cart taxis with the candy-striped canopies that patroled Mazatlán's main strip, keeping the flow of tourists as constant as the flow of cash.

"Hotel El Cid," Daguerre said.

"*Sí,*" the driver nodded with a yawn. "El Cid. Good hotel, *señor.*"

"I like it," Daguerre said from the back of the cart as it lurched forward. It was an odd sensation to be riding with his back toward the driver, watching where he'd been rather than where he was going. But it gave him a chance to make sure no one was following him.

Right now he didn't know what to think. There must have been some mistake, probably a grudge against the cousins, or an attempted robbery. Nothing to do with him. Surely he had just been at the wrong place at the wrong time. Not the first time in his life. But he had to be certain. After he changed into some dry clothes, he would plant himself next to his telephone until he got some answers.

Four minutes later they jerked to a stop in front of the El Cid. Daguerre climbed out of the cart and overtipped the driver. The driver looked at the wet money and nodded with another gaping yawn. "*Gracias, señor*. Good hotel."

Daguerre marched through the lobby and up to the front desk. Salt water dripped from his loose trunks down his muscular legs and formed little puddles on the tile floor.

"*Buenos dias*, Señor Daguerre," the young clerk smiled from behind rose-tinted glasses. "Having a pleasant stay?"

It was the same question hotel clerks around the world always asked, but this one always asked it with such intensity that Daguerre could never decide whether the kid was truly sincere or was just a damn good actor. Right now, he didn't care one way or the other. "Pretty good time."

The clerk's face collapsed with agonizing regret, as if Daguerre had just announced a death in the family. "Oh, Señor Daguerre. Only 'pretty good'? In Mazatlán one must have a marvelous time. A supreme time. You should try the disco down the street. Many women. American rock band." He tapped the lens of his rose-tinted glasses. "Glasses also American. The best."

"May I have my key, please? Room 16."

The young clerk snatched the key from its slot without looking. He flipped it over his back and caught it in his right hand, bouncing it in his palm as he spoke. "Very lively time at disco. Surfing music. Good food." He leaned forward and whispered, "Much better food than here. Fish fresher."

"I'll try it," Daguerre finally agreed.

The clerk flashed a wall of marble-white teeth. "*Bueno, bueno*. You will have a good time. Carlos promises." Carlos tossed Daguerre the key and winked.

Daguerre wound his way through the outdoor corridors, past the lush tropical gardens, past the giant Roman pool complete with ornate columns rising from the bottom of the pool, past the outdoor café and finally to his room.

Room 16.

He slipped the key into the door and entered with a relieved sigh. The room was cool, much cooler than the ninety-degree heat that steamed the thick humid air outside. He was glad he'd left the air conditioner on despite a twinge of guilt about wasting energy. He walked to the closet and pulled it open. Wearing only a pair of wet trunks, and having just stepped into a cool room, his skin tingled with goose bumps. He needed a quick hot shower and a change before hitting the phone.

He reached into the closet and pulled out a pair of blue seersucker pants. He tossed them onto one of the twin beds and opened the top drawer of his dresser.

That's when he knew.

It was an old trick, but it always seemed to work. His three LaCoste shirts with the little alligators on the chest were lined up perfectly. Blue on the bottom, yellow in the middle, green on the top. Just as he'd left them. The collars were flat and straight.

Definitely *not* as he'd left them.

It was a habit really. A little something left over from his days working the Warsaw and Moscow beats. Not that he'd expected anything here, not on this cushy assignment. Certainly not someone searching his room.

Yet before he'd left for the beach, he'd tucked under one side of the collar of the top shirt. A minor difference. Hardly noticeable. But someone searching the drawer, someone concerned with leaving everything as neat as he'd found it, would always straighten out that flipped-under collar, leaving the shirt neater than before. That was habit, too. Even if they didn't expect Daguerre to come back alive, they'd want things neat for the police.

So. Daguerre knew his room had been searched. He had only one question now. Was the searcher gone?

Or still in the room.

4

He needed a weapon. It would not be wise to search the room without one.

Daguerre snatched the green LaCoste shirt out of the drawer and flipped it onto the bed, next to his seersucker pants. He jerked opened the next drawer and removed a pair of underpants and socks, also tossing them onto the bed. Humming loudly, he walked slowly between the twin beds and flipped on the radio built into the night stand. The announcer introduced the singer in Spanish as that *artista internacional*. Then Tony Bennett's gravelly voice began to sing, "If I Ruled the World." Daguerre turned the volume a little louder.

There were only three places someone could hide: the closet, under the bed, or in the bathroom. He'd already been in the closet, so that was clean. Of course, it was possible that whoever had been here had done their job and was long gone by now. But Daguerre didn't want to risk his life on that chance. Not after what had happened earlier at the beach. Besides, he was almost hoping someone was still here. He wanted answers. Anyway he could get them.

But first, he wanted a weapon.

He walked casually back to the closet, singing along with Tony Bennett, deliberately hamming it up a little.

" 'If I ruuuled the world / Every daaay would be the first daaay of spring. . . .' " He reached into the closet and removed his sturdiest tie, a blue silk Pierre Cardin sent to him by his parents last month for his birthday. His mother's choice, no doubt, since his father was partial to loud plaids.

Daguerre continued singing boisterously as he slid open the dresser drawer. " '. . . not if I ruuuled the world.' That's a tough note, Tony. A little high for a bass like myself." He reached into the corner of the drawer under the row of balled-up socks. There he found what he'd been looking for.

His keys.

He didn't know why he always brought them on trips where they would do no good, except that he felt better having them with him. Reminding him he had a place to go to called home. With homey things not found in any hotel: Phillips-head screwdrivers, a fingerpainting by his goddaughter in second grade, a bathtub ring. It proved that he lived a part of his life not out of a suitcase, not chasing something. That he belonged somewhere.

It was a thick brass ring with fifteen keys to various doors and objects: his apartment in Santa Monica; his Avanti; the lock on his ten-speed Raleigh bicycle; his locker at the health club; his old briefcase that had burned up three years ago in a battle in Rhodesia, and several keys he wasn't sure about anymore.

Except one. One he would never use again, but he could not bring himself to throw out. The only key that fit something he really cared about. The one to Cara's one-room flat in Rome. Holding it in his hand right then, rubbing the thumb over the brass teeth, he remembered how she always looked delightfully surprised whenever he came through her door. Then he knew exactly why he still carried the ring with him everywhere.

He slipped the blue silk tie through the brass key ring and knotted it tightly. Wrapping the other end of the tie around his hand, he let the heavy end swing next to his leg. The weight felt good, formidable. Deadly.

The radio announced another *artista internacional* and Frank Sinatra began to sing "All the Way." Daguerre sang along loudly and out of tune as he strolled toward the bathroom. He'd already discounted the bed. To hide under the bed would have been too clumsy, too amateurish. And Daguerre had a feeling that the people he was dealing with were not amateurs.

The bathroom was dark, the door open about a foot. The shower curtain was closed.

Daguerre crept closer, each step bringing him into more of a crouch. His muscles were coiled so tightly they ached. He felt a ticking in his stomach, like an internal clock. Or a bomb. He'd entered jungle huts in Vietnam the same way, but with a camera instead of a gun. Moving slowly, holding his breath. Waiting for the bullet he'd never hear. Never write about.

He was less than two feet away from the bathroom door now. He took a deep breath. Released. Then exploded into movement like a sprung bear trap.

His shoulder smashed into the flimsy door, slamming it fully open. The cheap wood cracked and splintered, muffling another heavier sound. A thud. Then a groan.

Someone was behind the door.

Dagger banged into it again, but the man had already

jumped out from behind the door. Dagger saw the gun before he saw the man's face.

It was a Makarov pistol with a sound suppressor. Only 1.46 pounds unloaded, the compact little gun could fire 9mm bullets at 1,023 feet per second at a maximum effective range of 54 yards. Right now it was less than one yard away.

And it was pointed at Daguerre's bare chest.

The man with the gun pulled himself along the wall of the bathroom, clutching his own chest where the door had crashed into him. Daguerre recognized the face, or more precisely, the thick black mustache. It was the man from the motorboat. The one who had cut his line. The one who had knifed Fernando and Jesus.

The man was pointing his gun, trying to draw a deep breath. Something rattled deep in his chest whenever he inhaled. He sneered at Daguerre and thrust the gun farther out. Daguerre saw his finger begin to tighten around the trigger.

Go! he commanded his body, and everything moved at once. His legs leaped to the side, his head tucked into his neck, his right arm lashed out with the tie-and-key ring weapon. The serrated edges of the keys sawed the assassin across the back of his hand, slashing deep into the skin and crushing the fragile metacarpal bones. The gun dropped onto the bathroom floor and clattered against the toilet.

When the man lunged for the loose gun, Daguerre quickly swung his makeshift weapon around like a knight wielding an iron mace. It sliced through the air with a foreboding swoosh, raking the man down the side of his face into his mustache. Blood spurted from the clawlike wounds. He yowled, his hands flying helplessly to his ravaged face.

Daguerre swung again. The keys dug into the other cheek, ripping off six inches of pockmarked skin. The man sprawled backward into the wall. Ruts of blood streaked his face and bits of torn flesh clung to his cheeks like putty.

Daguerre lunged for the gun. But as he bent over, the assassin's foot suddenly swept around and kicked Daguerre's legs out from under him. He tumbled to the floor, his head cracking against the hard edge of the sink as he fell. Immediately his head throbbed as if it had split open. He heard distant popping sounds in his ears.

The man with the bloody face was moving again, crawling toward the gun. He rasped and rattled with each breath, each painful movement. His black eyes glowed fiercely with determination. Blood dropped from his chin.

Less than two feet away, Daguerre struggled to lift his tender head off the floor. It felt heavy and swollen like a bowling ball. Lazily he shifted his head to watch the other man. He didn't like what he saw.

The assassin's hand closed around the Makarov's handle, his finger hooked through the trigger guard. He wheezed, spat out slimy mucus mixed with blood, then swung the gun toward Daguerre.

But Daguerre had managed to raise himself far enough to flick his weapon into his attacker's face. The sharp metal keys jingled against the brass ring as they stabbed into the man's left eye. Blood squirted across the keys. The man screamed. His fingers convulsed and the gun went off.

The first bullet shattered the mirror over the sink, showering both men with triangular shards of glass. He was firing wildly now, his free hand clutching his blind eye as he growled with hate. Bright blood seeped from between his fingers.

The second shot nicked Daguerre's thigh, plowing across four inches of skin before torpedoing off into the wall. It burned, as if someone had just dragged a hot branding iron across the skin. Absurdly, Dagger was momentarily relieved that he hadn't been wearing his new seersucker pants, which he'd only worn once.

The heavy smell of sulfur filled the tiny bathroom. Daguerre didn't wait to see where the next shot might hit.

He sprang forward, grasping his tie at either end. He swung his elbow into the man's temple, dazing him, then looped the tie around his neck.

He yanked hard.

The man gurgled, tried to twist his gun into Daguerre's chest. But it was all happening too fast. Too much pressure. Not enough air.

There was a flurry of grasping hands, a single spasm with arched back and knees banging desperately against the toilet, feet scuffing across tile. Mouth open, gulping. Then it was over. The man's muscles relaxed, his bowels opened. Daguerre made a grim face, pinched the dead man's wallet from his pants and backed out of the room rubbing his own sore head.

Staggering to the dresser, he picked up the miniature Sony tape recorder he used for interviews and notes, and stabbed the Record switch. "Memo: write a note to mom and dad thanking them again for the tie."

He switched the recorder off and slowly, painfully

lowered himself onto the bed. He pressed the clean La-Coste shirt against the bleeding furrow on his thigh and switched on the recorder. "Expense account: one La-Coste shirt complete with bleeding alligator, $32.50."

He began emptying the dead man's wallet.

The radio announcer introduced that *artista internacional* Barbra Streisand, who began singing "Evergreen."

The wallet was fruitless. Eighty-three pesos, a driver's license, a condom, an obscene playing card with two naked women burrowing into each other. Just the usual. The license was made out to Cortez Duran. Twenty-six years old. The address was Mexico City.

Daguerre gingerly touched the back of his head. There was no blood there. Considering the amount of pain, he figured there ought to be at least a few drops for his trouble. He sighed and turned down the radio. "Sing it, Barbra, you wacky *artista internacional*."

Methodically he removed everything from the wallet, turned it over and shook it, just to make certain. Then he scattered the contents across the turquoise bedspread and examined each item again.

That's when he saw it.

It had been stuck to the back of the playing card, sandwiched between it and the driver's license in the yellowing plastic windows of the wallet. He held it up to the light, turned it over and read both sides.

He smiled his second smile of the day. "Well, Barbra, I'd say we have our first genuine clue."

5

"Carlos."

The young clerk pocketed the thick wad of tip money he'd been counting and turned around. White teeth bloomed between thin brown lips. "*Sí*, Señor Daguerre?"

"I've left some rather important papers spread around my room, so I'd prefer that no one goes in there. Including the maid."

"Of course, Señor Daguerre. As you wish."

Daguerre slid a five-dollar bill across the desk.

"Not necessary, Señor Daguerre," Carlos protested as he slipped the bill into his pocket almost before Daguerre's hand had let it go. "Ah, such nice clothes you wear, Señor Daguerre. American?"

"American by way of Taiwan and Korea."

"Yes, *sí*. American clothes very best. Brooks Brothers very snazzy. When I move to your country and open hotel, I wear only Brooks Brothers."

Daguerre started across the lobby, relieved that his thigh wound had been so minor. A little pressure and a bandage had stopped the bleeding, and he was no longer limping.

More important was staying alive until he figured out what the hell was going on. It was obvious now that he had been the target all along, and that the two Mexican cousins had just gotten in the assassin's way. But why? He wasn't working on any explosive assignment. Surely it couldn't have anything to do with a past exposé. Once an article is in print, the journalist is usually safe. So why was someone scalp-hunting in his vacation?

Whatever the reason, Dagger didn't want to go out of the hotel unarmed anymore. Carrying the gun was too dangerous. A tourist caught with an illegal firearm could expect to spend a lot of Christmases in prison. Fortunately, an additional search of the dead man's body had turned up a handy switchblade, which now nestled snugly in Dagger's pants pocket. And he had more than a passing familiarity with how to use it.

But there were other complications. Mainly, keeping anyone from entering his room until he disposed of the body. And figured out how to explain the bullet holes in the bathroom. He had even turned up the air conditioner to its maximum, hoping to slow down the body's decomposition. He did not want his neighbors complaining about strange smells. Well, he would worry about those details later. For now he had a lead to follow. A little white card that said—

"Mr. Daguerre?" a woman's voice called.

Daguerre turned around. A young woman of no more than twenty-four stood behind him with an earnest expression. Her long brown hair was slightly streaked with blonde as if it had been in too much salt water and hot sun. Or too near a bottle of hair coloring. It was getting harder for him to tell the difference.

Her face was long and angular, like a model's. So was her body. She was wearing cutoff jeans that had begun to fray and unravel up the side seams so the edge of her underpants peeked out just a little. They were yellow, Daguerre noted. Her top was a blue work shirt completely unbuttoned but knotted at the bottom. Underneath was a blue bikini top.

She also had an expensive Nikon camera slung over one shoulder, a tiny Panasonic tape recorder over the other, and a red canvas purse in her hand. A thin gold chain circled her left ankle and there was a Band-Aid around her big toe and another on her calf.

"Shaving and smoking." She grinned.

"Pardon?"

"Shaving and smoking. That's why the Band-Aids. I noticed you looking at them." She stuck out her shapely leg and also appraised the Band-Aids. "Kind of ugly, I know. Shaving and smoking. Bad combination."

Daguerre looked at his watch. "I'm sorry, but—"

She took another step closer, elbowing her camera and tape recorder out of the way. "You see, I'm giving up smoking. Slowly. I figure that's the most mature way. I mean, I'm not a fanatic, so I don't see why I should go cold turkey. So I've cut myself down to one cigarette a day. In the morning."

Daguerre looked over his shoulder. Carlos winked and nodded approval. Daguerre sighed. It would not do for him to be too abrupt with this woman. It might look suspicious. So, if he could just lead her outside it would be easier to get rid of her. Hop in a taxi and off he'd go. He started walking slowly toward the lobby door.

"Anyway," she continued, following closely behind him, "there I was sitting naked on the edge of the tub— which was a little cool first thing in the morning—

shaving my legs. That's when I decided to have my one cigarette of the day. Well, to make a long story short, while I was shaving, I nicked my calf. And when I opened my mouth to yelp, the cigarette pops out and rolls across the bathroom floor. But when I stand up to look for it, I step right on it with my big toe. Really burned it, too. A big blister. Ugh!'' She shook her head. "Crazy, huh?"

Daguerre held the lobby door open for her, then followed her outside. The sudden temperature change made his skin tingle. "It was nice talking to you," he said with his most charming smile, "but I really do have to be going."

She frowned. "Aren't you even curious as to how I know your name?"

Daguerre shrugged. Strange women knowing his name was not unusual. He was not totally unaware that some women found his lean chiseled features attractive, though he didn't consider that very important. Unless it could be used to help him get a story. He had often been approached by women who had asked a hotel employee about him, his name, room number.

"Well, some hotshot reporter you are." She shook her head in exasperation. "I thought you'd be a hell of a lot more curious than that."

This time Daguerre was surprised. "A reporter?"

"Uh-oh, here comes the big denial. 'Honestly, young lady, you must be mistaken. I'm a simple tourist.' Something like that, right? Well, it won't wash, pal. You're Christian Tulsa Daguerre. Formerly with the Kydd News Service. Now free lance. And you broke my heart."

Now Daguerre was suspicious. He had been trained never to forget a face or voice walk. To file each away for future reference when it could be used to get a story. Or even save his life. He studied her face again to make sure, shook his head. "Sorry, you're wrong. I would have remembered."

The young woman threw her head back and laughed. It was a deep, honest laugh, good-natured and sincere. Daguerre hadn't heard a laugh like that in a long time. It made him smile despite himself.

"I'd like to take that statement as a compliment," she said. "But I'm afraid I can't." She laughed again. "Maybe this will help that dazed look of yours. My name's Alexandra Kydd, daughter of you-know-who."

Daguerre's smile broadened. "Of course! You're Hannibal Kydd's daughter. I haven't seen you since—"

"The inauguration six years ago. You were covering the White House for one of daddy's papers, the *Washington Dispatch*. A few months before you quit and went free lance. What happened?"

"Your father and I had a disagreement."

"You and most of the civilized world. He can be pretty rotten sometimes. He always says you don't get points for being a nice guy." She shifted the camera out of her way. "I know something happened between you and dad back then, something awful. He won't talk about it and I figure you're too polite to say anything against him. I just wanted to tell you that I know what a terror he can be. But he's really not all bad, you know. I think it's just that he loves his work too much. More than people, you follow?"

Daguerre nodded, but said nothing.

"Anyway, I recognized you even if you didn't remember me."

"You were quite a bit different six years ago."

"Give or take a few inches."

"I'd say give."

She blushed slightly. "Thanks, I hope."

Daguerre checked his watch again. "Look, Alex, I'd like to chat some more, but I really am pressed right now. Why don't you give me the name of your hotel and I'll give you a call. We can finish our reminiscences over a proper Mexican dinner."

"No deal."

Daguerre looked surprised. "What?"

"I said no deal. You're not getting rid of me that easily, Chris. This is not just a social call you know."

"I don't understand."

"Do you think I lug all this crap around in this heat because I'm a zealous tourist? Hell, no. I'm a reporter, too. Just like you and dad. Well, all right, maybe not the same caliber, but—"

"Who are you reporting for?"

Alexandra Kydd squared her shoulders defiantly. *"The Answer."*

"Oh, no."

"Now, I know what you're going to say. That it's just a supermarket scandal tabloid that's only interested in which celebrity's boffing whose daughter. Or people who get kidnapped by UFOs. Well, damn it, so what? It's a start. And the pay's good. So I hang around celebrity driveways and snap photographs of some dumb TV soap star making it with an anchorman's wife. It could be worse." She grinned. "It could be daddy's anchorman's wife."

"But what are you doing down here?"

"I have a spy in my father's house. A source, I guess you'd call her."

"Yeah, who?"

She smiled. "My mother. She checked his office calender, saw your name and this address scrawled in that little hen scratching of his, and told me. So I left the painted turtle in Bakersfield who can cure cancer with a touch of his magic shell, and flew straight down here. My paper's furious with me."

"Look, Alex—"

"No, don't start. If you're down here then there must be some big hard news story that no one else knows about. I want in." She curled her lower lip between her teeth in an expression of determination. "It's my chance."

"I'm sorry to disappoint you, but I'm just here writing a travel piece on Mexico. I combined a little work with vacation. I don't know why your father's keeping tabs on me, but that's all there is to it. No hard news."

"Damn it, Chris, come off it. Daddy's been on my back for two years, ever since I graduated from Columbia. He keeps screaming for me to get into 'legitimate' journalism. But it's just not that easy. There are a lot of journalists around, and fewer and fewer newspapers."

"Can't your father help?"

She gave him a stony stare. "I don't want it that way. I don't want to succeed only because I'm Captain Kydd's daughter. I figured *you* would understand that."

Daguerre nodded. "I do, Alex. But I can't help you either. I really am on a travel piece."

"Don't con me, Chris. You haven't done a travel piece in ten years, since you were my age. I've followed your career very closely. Your stories on Soviet Gulags, with photos from the inside that no one has yet figured out how you got. Or that one on military stockpiling of biological weapons in Long Beach where you went in disguised as an Army general on inspection. If the Pentagon hadn't caught so much flak for what they were doing, they'd have roasted your butt for dinner. Now you're telling me that you're just down here to play tourist?"

"Yes, I—"

"Señor Daguerre," Carlos called as he came bursting through the lobby door. "Thank goodness you are still here. This message just came for you. Other clerk, Pedro, take the telephone call and stick message in box, but I saw you out here. Ran out." He panted slightly to demonstrate his effort.

Daguerre handed him a one-pound note. "English money okay, Carlos?"

"Tip not necessary, Señor Daguerre." Carlos smiled, snatching the bill from Daguerre's hand and giving him the folded message. He glanced appreciatively at Alex, smiled at Daguerre and disappeared back into the lobby.

"What's in the note?" Alex asked, reaching for it. "Something about your assignment?"

"None of your business." He quickly shoved it in his pants pocket unread. "Probably my editor wanting to move my deadline up a week."

"Sure, sure. Come on, give me a break. I can do research. Be your photographer. Deep background work. Anything. I'm good, Chris, really good. Just level with me."

Daguerre grabbed her roughly by the shoulders and let his dark eyes bore into hers. "I am telling you the truth, Alex."

Angrily she shook him free, her camera and tape recorder clattering against each other. "Fine. If that's how you want to play it. But I know you're on to something. Drugs maybe. Or worse. But whatever it is, I'll be there when it all goes down. I'm sticking to you like a bad sunburn, pal. Wherever you go, I go. From now on everything you say is on the record." She switched on the tape recorder and held it up to her mouth. "I'm standing in front of the Hotel El Cid on Avenida del Mar in Mazatlán, speaking to reporter Christian Tulsa Daguerre...."

But when she turned around again, Daguerre had already ducked into a waiting taxi. He was giving the driver an address. The address on the card he'd found in the dead man's wallet.

6

"Können Sie das Auto verlieren?"

The taxi driver looked at Daguerre in the rearview mirror and wrinkled his nose. *"Qué?"*

"You do not speak German?" Daguerre asked indignantly in a heavy German accent.

"No, *señor*. A little English."

"*Gut*, zat vill do. Can you lose zat automobile zat is following us? Ze white taxi?"

The driver twisted around to face Dagger. "Is this a movie, *señor*? Maybe we can start over again. I am sure I could give my lines better. More natural. Like Ricardo Montalban."

Daguerre sighed. "*Nein*, my friend. It is not a movie. It is my wife following me and—"

"Ah, *sí*. I understand everything. Leave it to me."

The driver punched the accelerator and the car lurched through the red light. Daguerre watched the white taxi hesitate at the light, then also leap through.

The sneaky brat must be paying off her driver, too. Daguerre groaned.

"Er, driver—"

"*Sí, sí,* I see them. Do not worry." Suddenly the car swept around the corner, tipping briefly onto its two left tires. There was a loud squeal and the pungent smell of burned rubber. Immediately they swung around another corner, this time tipping onto the right tires. More squealing. More burned rubber.

Daguerre looked over his shoulder through the back window. The white cab was still with them.

"Zey are still zere," Daguerre said.

The driver nodded philosophically. "*Sí*, my brother is a very good driver."

"Your brother?"

The driver shrugged and grinned into the mirror. "Just be thankful it is not my father, *señor*. He is eighty-three and drives so fast my brother and I will not ride with him."

Daguerre looked back at the white cab. He reached into his pocket for his cash, pulled out the folded message from Carlos along with his money. He peeled off a twenty-dollar bill. "Here's a souvenir from ze United States. A portrait of one of zere presidents, suitable for framing. Herr Andrew Jackson."

"*Sí, senor*, I know just the place to hang him."

Daguerre dropped the twenty onto the front seat next to the driver. It disappeared in an instant.

Immediately the car rocketed forward, screamed around a corner, shot up a hill, around another corner and continued winding through narrow streets, barely missing children and dogs.

Daguerre sat back against the torn vinyl seat and began unfolding the message Carlos had handed him. He had suspected it was merely a message from Danny at *West Coast*, perhaps complaining about the expenses or moving up his deadline. But when he finished opening the note, he found the last thing he would ever have expected.

Four words followed by a name and address.

Daguerre stared, his face suddenly ashen, drained of blood. His teeth ground against each other as his lip curled into a wolfish sneer.

Four words. Four simple words guaranteed to make Daguerre drop everything, change any plans. To risk anything. He studied the note again. The four words.

Cara's killer is here!

It was signed: Hannibal S. Kydd. Alex's father.

"Turn the cab around," Daguerre ordered, reading the address aloud to the driver.

The driver shrugged. "What about your wife, *señor*?"

"My wife," Daguerre nodded. "Yes, my wife. . . ."

Almost wife.

Cara.

CARA FRANCESCA CARLSON.

Rome.

"I like it when we're naked," she'd said.

Daguerre had glanced up from his shaving and smiled. She had winked back.

Less than a year ago. Ten months, seven days to be exact.

And Daguerre was exact. It was as if he had an inner clock that kept its own unforgiving time.

He had been free-lancing an article about the Jewish ghetto in Rome, a section of the lower east bank of the Tiber River close to Tiber Island. He'd spent the last two days strolling along the Largo Argentina, photographing the four small temples built there between the second and first centuries B.C. But today he was taking the day off to spend with his fiancée of two months.

"Did you hear me?" she called from the bed.

"No," he lied.

"I said I like it when we're naked."

"Is that your Swedish father or Italian mother talking?"

"Neither. It's me."

"Sex fiend."

She threw a pillow at his naked buttocks. He let it hit. "Hey, do you want me to cut my throat while I'm shaving?"

"Maybe a little. For love."

He stopped shaving and gave her a look that showed more love than he had ever spoken. She shivered deliciously under its intensity. He was good with words, too good sometimes, so she tended to trust his little looks more than his words. She loved his talent and mind, but she wasn't ashamed that she also loved his body. The hard muscular torso, the easy lope when he walked. The way other women looked at him. And his face. The dark blond hair and what she insisted was a Roman nose. He reminded her a little of that English actor, Michael Caine. A young Michael Caine.

"I mean it, about being naked. And I don't just mean sex. I mean, well, just how comfortable it is to be with you. As if I can trust you with anything. Any secret."

He wiped the patches of lather from his face and tossed the towel over his shoulder. "You have secrets?"

"Not yet," she teased, stepping out of bed with a movement so graceful Daguerre felt something tighten across his groin. At that moment he wished they'd been married for thirty years.

"Do you like this thing you do, what is it in English?"

"Free-lancing."

"Yes, free-lancing. Do you like this?"

"Yes," he answered, though he was concentrating on watching her walk across the room. She had her father's Scandinavian skin, pale, almost transparent. He could see blue veins pulsing across her breasts. She also had her father's height, six feet, most of which was legs.

"But your father is disappointed, no? He wanted you to be soldier."

Daguerre laughed. "Disappointed? I suppose. My father lived his whole life for the military. He was a colonel in the French army, won the Croix de Guerre, Medal Militaire, and the Legion d'Honneur. Did everything according to the book since he was seventeen. That is until he was stationed in Vienna after the war. That's where he met Lisa Durning with her boisterous Oklahoma drawl and her Kodak cameras always clicking. She was a photographer for *Look* magazine. Poor dad didn't have a chance. Giving in to the only impulsive act of his orderly life, he married her, retired from the service and moved with her from Vienna to Tulsa."

"Sounds romantic."

"It was. Except he hoped I would pick up where he left off. Tried to teach me everything he knew. Hand-to-hand combat. Strategy. Espionage. Codes. I couldn't get my allowance until I broke a coded message he'd give me every week. Even sent me to military school for a while, hoping I'd get a taste for it."

"Did you?"

"Not really. Oh, I liked the training, the knowledge. I was at the top of my class. But I hated the regimen, the structure. I like to do things my way."

"My little rebel," she smiled.

"You should have seen his face when I told him I wanted to be a journalist instead of a general. He looked like I'd just told him de Gaulle wore a garter belt. I tried to explain, told him I thought I could do more good as an observer, a writer."

"And now?"

"Now? Now he sees what I've done and he admits maybe I was right. Though he can't help suggesting that if I am such a good journalist, imagine what an even better general I'd have made. You can't win."

"One never can with parents. That is nature."

"Is that what our kids will say about us some day?"

"If we raise them properly, yes."

They finished dressing and headed for the door. Daguerre slung his Konica Hexanon Auto S2 over his shoulder.

"You promised no work today," Cara protested. "I promised not to grade papers and you promised none of your, um, free-lancing."

"This isn't for work. It's for pleasure. I want a few more shots of you so we'll have something to show the grandchildren how pretty you once were before your face got all pruny with wrinkles."

She swatted him playfully on the arm. "Rat."

He clicked off a few pictures of her as she chased him around the room.

"No buildings?"

"Just you."

They raced down the narrow stairs into the bright August sunlight, walking, laughing and hugging their way to the Via Nazionale to see the Piazza della Repubblica, the old city's youngest fountain.

As Daguerre shifted positions, constantly snapping pictures of Cara, she explained the fountain's history. Like most Romans, she was proud of her city's history and never passed up an opportunity to boast of its magnificence. "Did you know that this fountain originally was merely simple jets of water?"

"No, I didn't. Hold still."

"Yes, it was. It was dedicated by Pope Pius IX just ten days before the troops of united Italy stormed the city. All these sea beasts and nymphs weren't added until 1901."

"Amazing."

She laughed. "Go ahead, make fun of everything. Is that your French father or American mother?"

"Both."

"Okay, no more lectures about the glory that was Rome. I think you already know it all, anyway, better than I."

"I thought I did," he said, guiding her toward an outdoor café. "But this story I'm doing has added a neglected chapter in my education."

"What do you mean, Christian?"

"Did you know that until 1870, Jews in Rome were disbarred from any professions, government service and land ownership?"

"My God, that's terrible."

"And it all started with Pope Paul IV. It seems he—"

And those were the last words he would ever speak to her. If he had known, they wouldn't have been the ones he'd have chosen. But later he decided they were as good as any.

The screeching of tires was what interrupted Daguerre. The screeching of tires and the screaming of tourists who were standing nearby.

Two cars were responsible for the commotion. One was a beat up old green Citroën that had swerved sideways into the opposite lane of traffic. The other car was a shiny black Cadillac limousine that had been forced to the curb by the angle of the Citroën.

Suddenly everyone scattered.

The doors to the Citroën burst open and three husky men and a thin woman jumped out with their Walther P-38s already firing at the limousine. The Cadillac's windshield shattered in an explosion of glass, and the chauffeur's head collapsed under the barrage of bullets like a rotten melon. One bullet must have severed a neck artery, for a thin stream of blood was pumping through the missing windshield, splashing onto the hood of the car.

Daguerre had already flung Cara to the ground, covering her body with his own.

The back doors of the limousine were yanked open by two of the gunmen, while a third man reached in and violently dragged an elderly man out by the collar of his expensive suit jacket. The woman barked orders in Italian, then grabbed the elderly man's gray hair and helped drag him toward the Citroën, his knees and shoes scuffing across cement.

"*Avanti!*" she yelled at the other two. They abandoned the limousine and, with guns sweeping the crowd, stalked back to their car.

Daguerre ached to do something. But unarmed he was doing the most good right now, protecting Cara. In a few seconds they'd be gone, Cara would be safe and he could report the car's license number to the police.

But then everything went wrong.

All the people who'd been watching the kidnapping were huddled against buildings or lying flat on the ground. They waited without blinking, without breathing. For many, this was not the first kidnapping they'd witnessed. They knew Italy had become rampant with them in recent years. Most people, therefore, knew enough to just stay still and wait. And that's what they all did.

Except one.

Somehow, a small two-year-old toddler broke away from her mother, who had tried to contain all four of her children within her circled arms, shielding them. But the child ducked free and stumbled awkwardly toward the Citroën, laughing and pointing.

"Maria!" the mother shrieked with panic, releasing her other children as she ran for her daughter.

The sudden noise caused two of the men not yet in the car to snap around and open fire before they even knew what was going on. Bullets sprayed in a series of explosions and Daguerre saw the mother double over, her hands clutching her mangled stomach just as they had clutched her children. For dear life.

When Daguerre saw the gunmen leveling their weapons on the two-year-old girl who was running after her crumpled mother, he bolted. A bullet zinged off the pavement three feet from the little girl as Daguerre scooped her up in his arms and rolled away with her tucked safely under him.

The Citroën had started up and was beginning to roll. The panicky gunmen continued firing at anything that moved. But the only thing moving now were the other children—toward their fallen mother.

Cara watched with horror as the gunmen took aim at the children. Then, following her lover's example, she ran toward them to warn them back.

That's when it happened.

And Daguerre saw all.

He saw the 9mm parabellum bullet, traveling at 1135 feet per second, punch through Cara's back just below the left shoulder blade and spit out her chest where her heart used to be. Cara pitched forward, her soft face scraping ancient stone, dead before she fell. The white sweater she'd tied around her neck began soaking blood until it looked like a red cape.

The Citroën sped away.

Ten days after a million-dollar ransom had been paid for the elderly Italian businessman, his severed head was found in the men's-room sink at Rome's main library.

DAGUERRE read the message again.

Cara's killer is here!

He folded the paper carefully, as if it were a precious parchment, and tucked it back into his pocket. The poor son of a bitch lying dead in the hotel bathroom would have to wait. First he had to see Alex's father, Hannibal S. Kydd.

One son of a bitch at a time.

7

"Aren't you going to kill me?"

Dagger did not answer.

Hannibal S. Kydd shrugged, sipped his papaya juice. "That's what you said you would do to me next time we met, isn't it?"

"I said that's what I'd *like* to do."

"Well, son, we can't always get what we want, eh?"

"Thank you, Mick Jagger."

"Huh?"

"Forget it," Daguerre waved. "Before your time." He crossed the hotel room with a tense stride, as if he didn't know who to trust least, his host or his own anger. He pulled the folded message from his pocket. "Okay, you've got my attention, now what's the pitch?"

Kydd laughed, a raspy choking laugh. "You know me too well, Dagger. Too damn well. Nothing for nothing, right? Give and take in this business. That's what I taught you." He gulped another mouthful of papaya juice, swirled it around in his mouth a while, then swallowed. "Drink? I've got orange juice, papaya juice, mango juice, pineapple juice, apple juice. Hell, I got any kind of juice you could name. And all fresh. No canned shit."

"Nothing," Daguerre said, sitting on the sofa. "Just names and addresses."

"Soon. We haven't worked out our deal yet."

Daguerre felt his blood pulsing through his arms and legs, his anger pushing at his chest, throbbing in his brain. But he waited. Kydd was not the kind of man to be hurried. And he could take a punch, as Dagger had proven before.

"You haven't changed much, Dagger. Maybe a little harder looking around the eyes. But still the easy charm of a gigolo."

"You haven't changed either, Captain. If you don't count the extra twenty pounds hanging around your gut. But I guess you've compensated for that by allowing your bald spot to cover your whole head now. Clever move."

Kydd chuckled. "Like old times, eh?"

"No, Captain. There were no old times. Remember?"

Kydd said nothing, merely drained the last of his papaya juice, licked his lips.

Hannibal S. Kydd. Captain Kydd, they called him. Like the pirate. "They" being anyone who'd ever done business with him, including a couple of presidents and an assortment of senators and other politicians. It was not a term of affection.

Hannibal Kydd had inherited his father's rural newspaper when he was twenty-one. The *Fargo Sun-Gazette*. North Dakota's finest. Circulation: 45,000. In thirty years he had parlayed that tiny hayseed business into an international conglomerate that owned twenty-eight newspapers, a wire service, sixteen television stations,

twelve radio stations and five magazines. He was one of
the most powerful men in the country, but he was still a
newsman. Willing to hire the best reporters, spend any
amount, bully the most powerful politicians—just to get
the story. Yet despite his huge electronic empire, he also
liked to go down to watch the presses roll, swap stories
with the men who ran the presses, come back home with
fresh ink smeared on his face and clothes.

But he was not just some rube playing in the big time.
He knew how to fix a multimillion-dollar press with a
pair of pliers and a screwdriver, but while he was doing
it he could also quote you the latest Q ratings, discuss
current discoveries in the computer industries, and buy
and sell currency on the international market.

Yet there had been a price for all this. It had happened while he was still owner-editor of the *Washington
Dispatch*, long before Daguerre had gone to work there,
before Daguerre had even started college. It was the
middle of a truckers' strike, four weeks old and hardly
anything in the country was moving. Management had
made an offer and a straw poll of the strikers indicated
they were ready to accept. But the union negotiators refused. They wanted more. It was then that Hannibal S.
Kydd ran a story under his by-line concerning the de-
pleted pension fund of the union, which was why they
were holding out for so much money. The strike ended,
a Senate investigating committee was formed, a couple
of flunkies went to jail.

And Hannibal S. Kydd had a small mustard jar full of
sulfuric acid thrown in his face.

Daguerre stared at the man now as Kydd poured himself another glass of papaya juice. He was short, no

more than five-four, thick everywhere: neck, arms, middle. But he never looked fat, just dominating. There were wisps of rusty hair here and there, but mostly his head was freckled skin. And over his eyes he wore black wraparound sunglasses that hugged his face and blocked out all light. Seeping out from under the left lens was a bone-white patch of scar tissue, thick and wrinkled like molten plastic where his face had sizzled and melted. The left eye was blind. The right eye was weak, sensitive to light. It, too, was inlaid in a bed of scars, like a precious jewel in a battered bronze ring. But those scars were from the thirty-two operations that allowed him to see anything at all. And doctors still weren't certain how long that would last.

"I was sorry to hear about Cara," Kydd said. "She was a fine lady."

"Yes, she was. Now if you know where the slime who killed her are, tell me."

"First things first, Dagger."

"Meaning business."

"Right. I want the exclusive."

Daguerre's mouth twisted into an imitation of a smile. "For what I'm going to do to them, I certainly don't want to tell the world."

"I don't want the facts, man, I want the truth."

Daguerre sighed. "We aren't going through this again, are we, Captain? That's why I quit you in the first place. I didn't like the chances you took with your reporters' lives. Especially after Sharon Duvall and Bill Aimes were killed."

"Hell, *you* take risks all the time. Vietnam. You sneaked into a rescue squad going after POWs, parachuted into enemy territory and ended up pulling three guys out of that camp yourself when most of the squad was killed. Hell, they even wanted to give you the damn Congressional Medal of Honor until you made me convince them not to."

"I'm a journalist, not a soldier. The medals belong to the soldiers. They do that sort of thing every day. We're only the observers."

"Bullshit, Dagger. There are no observers in this world. Cara was an observer, yet she ended up a casualty."

Daguerre's throat tightened. "She knew the risks. So did I. But Sharon and Bill didn't. You sent them into an explosive situation without fully informing them of the dangers. People should have the right to decide when they want to gamble their lives. Isn't that what we're all fighting for?"

"Maybe," Kydd muttered, looking into his glass of papaya juice. For a moment his face sagged with regret. Then he looked up again, his mouth firmly set. "But I built my papers to stand for something. You have your survival skills and I have mine. And mine mean getting the damn story. Period. Now I have some information on someone involved with Cara's death. If you want it you deal with me. Otherwise, there's the door."

Daguerre waited.

"That's better. You know me, Chris. You know I'm not a hard guy, not with people I care about. But this whole terrorist situation stinks and somebody's got to do something about it. The government's hands are tied up in so many knots we're lucky if they even admit publicly that terrorists exist. Fortunately, I've got the money, the connections, the power to do something about it. I can find them, keep after them, overturn every rock they hide under and shine a public spotlight on them. It's not much, but it's a goddamn start.''

''That's not journalism, that's a crusade.''

''And what you want to do to the scum who killed Cara, what's that called?''

''Revenge. But I don't claim it's anything else.''

Kydd shook his head sadly, set his glass on the table. ''I expected more from you, Chris.'' He reached up, grabbed the rims of his sunglasses and slowly removed them. The left eye socket was empty, a flap of twisted skin and lumpy scar in a sunburst pattern where the acid had splashed against his face. The right eye was criss-crossed with surgical scars, the eye itself red and wincing from the light, struggling to stay open as it glared at Daguerre.

''Go ahead. Look at it. You talk about revenge. Well, I know something about it, too. The people who did this were terrorists, in their way. I wanted to kill them and the bosses who ordered it, and the judges who let these people off with minor sentences. I could have killed a hundred people and still not felt satisfaction. Revenge is fine, it's a place to start. But it's not an end. The real satisfaction isn't just in killing them, it's in preventing them from hurting someone else. And that difference can keep you from becoming just like them. Think about it, Chris.'' He slid the glasses back in place.

Daguerre stood up, went to the portable refrigerator behind the fancy mahogany bar and poured himself a glass of orange juice. ''Why me, Captain? You know we don't get along.''

"We did once."

"That was two lives ago. Bill's and Sharon's." He sat the untouched juice on the counter. "Besides, you've got dozens of excellent reporters working for you. Real aces."

"This isn't in their league and you know it. We're not talking about corrupt politicians here. We're talking maniacs with guns who'd as soon kill you as tell you their favorite color. You've got the background, and I don't mean just journalism." He held out his glass and let Daguerre fill it with orange juice. "You went through six weeks of Special Forces training with the Green Berets for that article you did for me. Remember? Colonel Sharpe said you were one of the best soldiers he'd ever seen. A natural. Your dad and I had a laugh over that. And speaking of your dad, let's not forget that he personally trained you in small arms and combat since you were a brat. Hell, Dagger, you've had more military training than a dozen soldiers. And that's what it's going to take."

"What's the information you have?"

Kydd shrugged his beefy shoulders. "Not a hell of a lot. You already know the kidnappers who killed Cara were Red Brigades. But one of them wasn't Italian. He was a supervisor from the PLO. He planned the whole operation, including the execution of the industrialist they kidnapped."

"PLO, huh? That explains the sloppiness."

"Yeah. But it was successful in terms of getting the million dollars. And they all escaped. So sloppy or not, the bastard got a promotion and is now the big enchilada in Latin America."

"Specifically?"

"Specifically Mexico. At least he was last seen here."

Daguerre felt a chill scraping along his spine. He'd never been this close before. "How clean is this information?"

"Scrubbed and polished. CIA. We made a little swap. I killed a story on their budget excesses in exchange for what they had."

"Are they involved?"

"Nope. Passive surveillance. Observers."

Daguerre caught the dig, ignored it. "What else?"

"Not much. They only know his code name. Centaur. Like in mythology. Half horse's ass, half man. It's the half that's man you have to watch out for."

"Where'd they last see him?"

"That's the odd part. Saw him at a travel agency. One in Acapulco, one here in Mazatlán. Different branches of the same agency."

Daguerre pulled out the card he'd taken from the dead man in his hotel room. "The Maya Agencia de Viajes."

"My God, how'd you know that?"

"They tried to cancel my reservation."

Kydd looked shaken as he shifted uncomfortably on the sofa. "I didn't think...."

"You didn't think they'd act so quickly, right?"

Kydd nodded guiltily.

"What exactly did you do this time, Captain?"

"I sent the word out through the local underground that you were coming to Mazatlán. A big-time investigative reporter snooping around, looking into the travel agency for some unknown reason. I figured when I told you that, it might force you to take the assignment. I didn't expect them to try anything so soon, at least until I had a chance to warn you."

Daguerre's face was hard, glacial. "Which means you probably are behind my getting this travel assignment in the first place. A little pressure on *West Coast* magazine, right? Right?"

Kydd didn't answer.

Daguerre walked across the plush salmon carpet to the hand-carved oak door. When he spoke his voice was crisp yet hollow, as if it was returning after being bounced off the moon. "You got two kids killed today, Captain. Eighteen years old. Two more casualties for your private war. You see, that's what I mean about the gung-ho way you operate. It's too dangerous for the innocent bystanders. And that makes you too much like the enemy."

"Okay, Chris, I was wrong. I got excited and I went about it half-cocked. But you're going to need me to pull this all off. You're going to need my help, my influence, my—"

"How's your daughter doing these days, Captain?"

"Alex? She's in Beverly Hills playing at journalism. Snapping photos of Ryan O'Neal's bare ass or something. Why? What's she got to do with anything?"

But Daguerre had already closed the door behind him.

8

Even the building looked sinister, evil.

Just looking at it made Daguerre's muscles tense.

There on Avenida Aquiles, hunched between a boarded-up fruit-juice stand and a discount appliance store that hadn't washed its windows in at least a year, was the cramped office of the Maya Agencia de Viajes. A simple travel agency.

Daguerre took the card from his wallet and studied it. Just an ordinary business card, not unlike Daguerre's own, though he rarely carried them anymore. Printed on the front was the name of the travel agency, the address, the phone number. And then the strange part. In the bottom right-hand corner, the list of branch offices. They had locations in Cancun, Guadalajara, Puerta Vallarta, Mexico City, Tijuana and Acapulco.

From his vantage point across the street, Daguerre stared at the office with a confused frown. The building was shabby, and the tour prices advertised in the window were outrageously high. The huge plate-glass window, with the agency's painted name peeling off, was even filthier than the appliance store's window next door. There were no chairs inside for customers to sit down. Only a counter like a car-rental office. Behind the counter leaned a grizzled old man smoking a cigarette and reading a newspaper. Daguerre watched the store for ten minutes; no one went in or came out.

And why would they? It was the last place anyone anxious to plan their once-a-year vacation would go. Who would want to give their savings to such a seedy establishment? It was almost as if they *discouraged* business. Which lead Daguerre to ask another question: how could this agency not only remain in business, but afford to open so many other offices?

Daguerre flipped the small white card over in his hand. On the back were words scrawled in smudged pencil: *Christian Daguerre. El Cid, No. 16*.

He absently brushed the card against his lips as he stared at the tiny office across the street. It all centered around this run-down hole in the wall; the terrorist called Centaur, who was responsible for Cara's death; Cortez Duran, who had tried to kill Daguerre twice today. At least he now knew why they'd tried to kill him; Hannibal Kydd had spread the word that Daguerre was down here investigating the travel agency. They'd panicked. But why?

Hannibal Kydd was right about one thing. Daguerre could no longer remain merely an observer, a reporter of events. He knew that now, had suspected it for quite some time. Just standing there that close to where Centaur had been, might still be, made his body ache for action, not only for Cara's sake, but for the sake of everyone he might yet harm. It was no longer a world where knowledge or truth was enough. Something had to be done with that truth, someone had to do it. Right now that someone was Daguerre.

"Say 'marry me' for the camera," Alex said, running

up and snapping a picture of Daguerre's startled face. "Gotcha," she giggled.

"What in hell—"

She clicked on her Panasonic recorder and spoke into the condenser microphone. "This is your on-the-spot reporter Alexandra Kydd. Here I am again with Christian Tulsa Daguerre, standing on the scenic Avenida Aquiles. Mr. Daguerre, could you tell our readers why—"

Daguerre snatched the recorder from her hand, popped the miniature cassette out, slipped it into his pocket and tossed the recorder back to her. "If you put in another tape I'll smash it."

"Hey, First Amendment, remember?"

"Don't give me that crap, Alex. I'm a reporter, too."

"Yeah," she fumed, "so was Genghis Khan."

Once again Daguerre found himself smiling despite himself, despite the situation at hand, despite what he had to do. This woman was infectious. " 'So was Genghis Khan'? What's that supposed to mean?"

She laughed. "I don't know. It sounded great though, didn't it?"

He shook his head, grinned. "How'd you find me?"

"Simple. Once you lost me, I had my driver get in touch with your driver. They're—"

"Brothers."

"Right. Not only that, but Carlos, the hotel clerk at the El Cid, is their nephew."

"That explains their fondness for cash."

"For ten bucks your driver told us where you'd gone, but by the time I got to that hotel there was no easy way to find you again. So I took a chance, asked him where your original destination had been before you'd changed it, and came here. Miss me?''

Damn. He cursed himself. He hadn't expected such resourcefulness and tenacity from her. He'd have to stop thinking of her as the bratty seventeen-year-old she used to be and start remembering she had a lot of her father in her. And a lot of Hannibal S. Kydd was dangerous.

''Look, Alex,'' he said, ''I know you think I'm on some nasty undercover investigation, but you couldn't be more wrong. You can call my editor at *West Coast* magazine. Charge the call to me. They'll tell you that I'm just doing a simple travel piece.''

She snorted. ''Of course that's what they'd *tell* me.''

''It's the truth.''

''Why are you doing this to me, Chris? Why are you blaming me for whatever it is my father did? It couldn't have been that horrible.''

Dagger turned away, remembering. Horrible didn't even begin to describe what happened to Bill Aimes and Sharon Duvall.

''Mis-tah Christian, I presume?'' Bill Aimes grinned, perching his buttocks on the edge of Dagger's desk. ''How's tricks with Captain Bligh?''

''That's Captain Kydd,'' Sharon Duvall reminded him for the hundredth time. It was a little game they played. ''You're getting your movies mixed up again.'' She plopped into the chair next to Dagger's desk.

''Drop in any time, guys,'' Dagger said, fingers perched over his computer keyboard. ''My deadline's not for another fifteen minutes anyway.''

Bill snorted. "Don't hand us that sob story, Chris. Kydd treats you like the Second Coming of Edward R. Morrow. If you're late with your story it'll only prove to him you're human like the rest of us working slobs."

"Besides," Sharon added, lighting a cigarette to annoy Bill, "Captain Kydd would like nothing better than to barrel through the newsroom shouting, 'Stop the presses! Stop the presses!' "

They all laughed.

Dagger and Bill played squash together every Monday and Wednesday afternoon, loser buying lunch afterward. Bill Aimes had bought a lot of lunches. Sharon was new to the *Dispatch*, fresh out of Temple University with the ink on her diploma still drying. She was still at the stage of acting tough because she thought it was expected of women reporters. But she was a striking beauty with dark hair and eyes and a figure still trim from Temple's women's volleyball team. The very first week she had started at the paper, Bill had jokingly wagered with Dagger. "Winner gets to ask her out first," he had said. After the game he'd stumbled from the court panting, "I don't care, I'm still asking her out first."

He had, and since then they'd teamed up on special stories whenever possible. And after hours every night.

"What are you up to tonight, Chris?" Bill asked.

"A date with Tricia."

"Nixon?"

"Very funny. Tricia Phelps from the *New York Times*. We're either going out to see *Saturday Night Fever* or staying at home to watch "Roots." I'm pushing for staying home."

"God," Sharon sighed elaborately, "that could have been me if Bill hadn't beat you that day at squash."

Bill and Dagger exchanged glances; Bill hid his smile behind his hand.

"What about you two? Hot night on the town?"

Sharon shook her head. "Nope. Still working on that assignment for the Captain."

"Careful, Sharon," Bill warned with mock seriousness. "It's still a secret. Even from Golden Boy here."

Dagger smiled, but he was a little annoyed. Hannibal S. Kydd kept few secrets from Dagger anymore. It was obvious to everyone at the paper that he was being groomed to take over the paper first, and later the rest of the Kydd empire. Why then this "secret" assignment? Something about it nagged at Dagger.

"Well, if you two are on assignment, get your butt off my desk."

Bill pretended to be insulted, lifted one leg and made a farting noise with his mouth.

"Bill!" Sharon gasped, giggling uncontrollably.

Dagger laughed. "That'll cost you tomorrow on the squash court, buddy."

"Yes, suh, Mistah Christian." Bill saluted and led away a laughing Sharon.

Eight hours later Dagger's phone jangled him from his sleep.

"Yeah?" he mumbled into the phone.

"Hey, Chris, it's Billingsworth." Night reporter at the *Dispatch*. His voice was pinched and solemn, as if he wished he were somewhere else.

"What's up?"

A long pause. "I think you'd better come down here."

"What's it about?"

"Bill Aimes and Sharon Duvall."

"Where are you?"

"Morgue."

Dagger started dressing.

Tricia Phelps sat up in bed wide awake, a veteran of many late-night calls. "Want me to go with you?"

He shook his head. "I want what's going to happen next to be off the record."

Dagger sat in the tiny waiting room that was decorated like a dentist's office. The blank TV screen stared back at him. The deputy coroner stood on one side, Billingsworth was chain smoking on the other side.

"The female," the deputy coroner said into the microphone.

An image appeared on the screen. But even television couldn't sanitize the damage. Her skin was grayish, drained, the pretty young features somehow grotesque in death. Two small wounds punctured her face: one in the forehead, one in the cheek.

"Twenty-two caliber?" Dagger asked.

The deputy coroner nodded. "Execution style, except that they usually only need one shot. Probably breaking somebody new in."

"That's Sharon Duvall," Dagger said.

The deputy coroner spoke into the microphone. "Show us the male, Johnny."

The screen went blank a few seconds, then Bill Aimes face filled it up. The same small wound pierced his forehead. His face looked pale and disappointed, as if death wasn't at all like he'd expected.

"Bill Aimes," Dagger said, rising. He turned and marched out the door.

"Wait a second, Mr. Daguerre," the deputy coroner called. "There are still some questions."

"You bet there are," Dagger growled. "And I know just who to ask."

The forty-minute drive to Hannibal S. Kydd's Virginia mansion did nothing to cool Dagger's temper. If Kydd had any inclination of Dagger's mood, he didn't seem worried. The sentries at the front gate phoned Kydd directly and received instructions to let him through.

Jerome Earl, Kydd's driver-bodyguard answered the front door.

"Where is he, Jerry?" Dagger asked.

"Whoa there a sec, Chris," Jerome said, placing a beefy hand on Dagger's chest. At six-four and 280 pounds, Jerome Earl loomed over Dagger with muscles as dense as a black hole. Not to mention the .38 S & W riding his shoulder holster. "Let's just calm down first, okay?"

"I'm calm," Dagger said, brushing Jerome's hand away as he stalked toward Kydd's study.

"Don't be that way, Chris. Don't make me hurt ya." Jerome clamped his huge hand on Dagger's shoulder and spun him around. "He'll see ya when *he's* ready."

Dagger sighed. He liked Jerome, a tough, conscientious, former NYPD detective who played a thoughtful game of chess. But Dagger didn't want to play by Hannibal Kydd's rules tonight. Not tonight.

Again, he twisted out from under Jerome's grip and headed for the study.

"Aw, shit, Chris," Jerome lamented as he dug his hard fist into Dagger's kidney.

Dagger dropped to one knee, pressing the bruised kidney with his hand. He let Jerome come around in front of him and reach down to lift him to his feet before moving. When Jerome's head was bending close to his, Dagger snapped an uppercut into Jerome's jaw, following it with a left hook to the cheek and a right cross to the temple. Jerome stumbled backward, tripping over one of the fancy Persian rugs that lined the hallway.

Without hesitating, Dagger bolted through the tall double doors that lead to Kydd's study, locking them behind him.

"I didn't know you went in for such theatrical entrances, Chris," Kydd said from behind his massive desk. He was eating from a plastic cup of yogurt. "It's a good thing my wife and daughter are in New York this week."

Jerome's heavy fists were pounding on the double doors, echoing through the room like cannon blasts. "You sucker-punched me, ya bastard!"

Kydd chuckled. "He should have expected that. But then Jerome doesn't know you like I do. Doesn't know what you'll do to win. Like me."

"Not like you," Dagger scowled.

A pained expression crossed Kydd's face and Dagger was surprised now deeply he must have hurt him. He almost regretted it, until he remembered Bill and Sharon's dead gray faces.

"Bill Aimes and Sharon Duvall won't be coming into work tomorrow. Seems they've got their own TV show now. Live from the morgue."

The only light in the room came from the lamp on Kydd's aircraft-carrier-sized desk. The thick shadows it cast on his jowly face made him look older, tired. He adjusted his wraparound sunglasses. "I know about Bill and Sharon. Terrible tragedy."

"What were they working on?"

He spooned some yogurt into his mouth, chewed. "Nothing important. Consumer affairs."

"Bullshit."

The pounding on the door continued. "Goddamn it, Chris, I'll bust down this fucking door if you don't let me in."

Kydd threw his spoon across the room in one of the few times Dagger had ever seen him show anger. The spoon bounced off the door, leaving a splotch of yogurt. "Shut up and go to bed, Jerome!"

The pounding stopped. There was no other sound.

"What was their assignment?"

"I told you. Consumer affairs. They were looking into a mail-order company."

"Which one?"

Kydd hesitated, pulled his silk robe tighter as if against a sudden chill. "Lido, Inc."

"Jesus."

"They were just supposed to check on some complaints about mail fraud and bribery, that's all."

"Did you tell them that we had information linking Lido to the Mafia?"

Kydd didn't reply.

"Did you tell them that the place was a front for mail-order kiddie porn?"

"It wasn't necessary. They weren't supposed to be investigating that aspect of it. I didn't want them going in with any preconceptions.''

Dagger lunged over the desk, hauling Kydd out of his leather chair by the lapels of his silk robe. The cup of yogurt tumbled to the floor. "You sent them in to investigate mob holdings without telling them what they were up against. It got them killed, you son of a bitch." And Dagger socked Hannibal S. Kydd in the mouth.

Kydd flopped back into his chair, propelled by the force of the punch. He dabbed his fingers against the split lip and swollen cheek, winced, but didn't say anything. No protest, no threats, no complaints.

Dagger turned and left. That was the last time he'd seen Hannibal S. Kydd until a few minutes ago.

Since then Kydd had often tried to rehire him, had offered outrageous salaries, positions, power. But Dagger never answered a letter or returned a phone call. He even heard Kydd had established a generous scholarship at Temple University in Bill and Sharon's names.

There was a sadness to the whole incident for Dagger. He had lost not only two friends, but someone even closer. Someone he'd loved like a father.

"C'MON, DAGGER, don't toss me out just because I'm Captain Kydd's daughter. Give me a chance. I'm not afraid of a little danger."

"But I am. Now beat it."

"Jesus, you're just like dad."

That's what Kydd had said that night. That they were alike. That they both wanted to win. But there was more to it than just winning. There was being on the right side, the side that deserved to win because it stood for something worth fighting for.

"I don't care what you say," Alex proclaimed stubbornly. "I'm staying right here with you."

Daguerre swung around to face her, his eyes glaring. "Get the hell lost! Do you understand me now? Get away from me, you stupid bitch!"

Alex stumbled back a few steps, startled, frightened. She couldn't speak.

Daguerre continued to glare menacingly at her. He felt sorry for her, a little ashamed of himself, but it was for her own protection. "Beat it! Haul ass!"

She took a few more steps backward and disappeared around the corner of a brick bank building. Daguerre could hear her camera and tape recorder clattering as she ran.

He swallowed. That last shout had scratched his throat. But it had been worth it. She was gone. Now he could get on with it.

He started across the street in his usual manner, dodging the cars with ease, ignoring the Spanish curses and oaths hurled from irate drivers. But when he reached the opposite curb there was one voice he couldn't ignore.

"Hey, Dagger," Alex shouted from across the street, her camera pointed at him, a warble in her voice as if she'd been crying. "Stick it in your ear!" She clicked off half a dozen rapid photos of Daguerre framed by the Maya Agencia de Viajes behind him.

Then she was gone, back around the corner of the bank.

Daguerre pivoted back toward the agency, saw the old man pointing a bony finger at him, talking anxiously to two thick-necked Mexicans in cheap wrinkled suits. One had completely removed his tie, the other had merely loosened his knot a few inches. Both nodded at the old man and hurried into a back room closing the door behind them.

Daguerre entered.

A little brass bell jangled over the door. The old man stared at his newspaper with a bored expression. Daguerre had a feeling it was the only expression the old man ever had.

"Nice place," Daguerre said in fluent Spanish.

The old man looked up from his newspaper, took a puff of his cigarette. "If you say so," he said in English.

Daguerre kept his eye on the door through which the two burly Mexicans had gone. He didn't want any surprises. He stayed close to the front door.

"Not too busy today," Daguerre said.

"Busy enough. Too busy, maybe."

Daguerre took out the business card he'd removed from the dead man's wallet and tossed it on the old man's newspaper. It landed facedown, with his name, hotel and room number showing.

The old man took a deep draw on his cigarette, as if he hadn't even noticed the card. But Daguerre saw his eyes flicker a moment. Saw them glance out the dirty window into the street.

Daguerre looked too. The two burly Mexicans were there. One was behind the wheel of a battered green VW bug, the other was pointing at the bank. Then they both took off around the corner, one in the car, the other running on foot.

It wasn't him the old man had been pointing at before, Daguerre suddenly realized. It was Alex. Alex and that damned camera.

Daguerre yanked the door open, the tiny bell jangling hysterically, and dashed across the street, his shoes slapping pavement with an urgent beat. His hand reached into his pocket as he ran, closing around the switchblade.

As he spanked around the corner, he saw them. He pressed the button on the knife handle and the six-inch blade sprang rigid, locking open with a hungry click.

But it looked like Daguerre was already too late.

9

First he saw the blood.

Some dripped from a nasty gash across Alex's cheek, some leaked from her nose. More oozed over her split lower lip, already purple and swollen.

Yet still she fought, claws flashing, teeth snapping, legs kicking.

The man with no tie was slapping her repeatedly, forcing her toward the edge of the curb. There his partner sat behind the wheel of the VW bug, revving the engine and holding the passenger seat folded forward as they tried to stuff Alex into the back seat. The driver leaned across the folded seat and snagged Alex's wrist, pulling her toward him while his partner pushed her from behind, his hands lingering on her buttocks and crotch.

Alex continued to claw and scream, but the two men were too powerful. Still, she managed to slow them down, stomping on the foot of the man behind her. Angry and frustrated, he reacted by punching her sharply in the spine. Alex sagged to her knees with a moan.

That's when Daguerre reached them.

"Chris," Alex gasped, thick drops of blood spraying from her raw lips as she spoke. "Help me, Chris."

Daguerre charged ahead, his borrowed switchblade

held flat and low, street style. But the man with no tie was ready, spinning suddenly at Alex's cry and catching Dagger's wrist in both his huge hands. He twisted and wrenched, trying to force Daguerre to release the knife. But Daguerre held on, maneuvering around the burly man for a hip throw. But before he had the chance, the bigger man wrestled them both off balance and they sprawled to the pavement. They landed in a heap with the deadly point of the knife digging straight into the concrete sidewalk. Under the pressure of their combined weight, the blade snapped at the handle, shooting the broken tip out into the street. Both men scrambled to their feet.

Daguerre was first to his feet, quickly delivering a swift roundhouse kick to No Tie's lower back. He groaned loudly, his back arching with pain. Daguerre jumped closer.

No Tie, still smarting from the blow to his back, swung a lazy left hook that Daguerre easily ducked, firing off three short jabs of his own into No Tie's ribs. He could feel the ribs buckling under his hammering knuckles. No Tie staggered backward, one hand clasped over his aching ribs as the other hand dived inside his jacket for his gun.

Daguerre didn't wait. He attacked again, legs and hands twirling like blades of a windmill ran amok. First he sent a spinning kick to the wrist that sent the emerging gun flying halfway down the block. Then a left jab smashed the cheek and a right cross rammed the heart. The man gagged once, then collapsed backward onto the sidewalk, coughing, gasping for air.

"Chris! *Help*!"

Daguerre pivoted to see the man behind the wheel pulling Alex the rest of the way into the car. She was still struggling, but weakly. The driver glimpsed his fallen partner, panicked and quickly clubbed Alex on the back of the head. She slumped down to the floor of the VW and he gunned the engine. The car jumped forward, the passenger door still flapping open.

Daguerre ran after the car, praying for the traffic to slow the car down enough for him to catch up. But right now the street was fairly free of traffic, and the VW started to pick up speed. He ran alongside, only a couple feet from the swinging open door. If he could just grab ahold.

He reached out. No good. Too far.

He ran faster, his legs chewing up pavement like steam pistons. Now he was only a couple inches away. Pedestrians who had watched the fight, some even snapping photographs, stood by and cheered him on as he raced after the car. His legs were pumping so fast he wasn't sure he'd be able to stop them when he wanted to. His heart thumped in his ears. His mouth tasted metallic. He gulped air like a thirsty man would water. But still he ran harder. Almost there.

He reached out for the swinging door. His fingers grazed the chrome edge, touched the metal handle. Speeding up, he readied himself to leap through the open door. Just a few steps more. But when he looked into the car, he saw the driver pull out a gun, identical to the one No Tie had, and aim it at him. Daguerre immediately veered away from the car just as the first shot fired, shattering a plate-glass window of a pet

store behind him. Someone inside screamed. Dogs
barked.

Daguerre lost control. He tried to stop his legs, but
the momentum still carried him forward into a parked
car, where he thudded against the fender and rolled
across the trunk, slamming down hard onto the concrete
sidewalk. The rough pavement sandpapered the skin
from his palms, embedding pebbles and dirt in his torn
hands. He sprang up in time to see the green VW squeal
around a curb, its open door whacking a parked car,
ripping free and somersaulting through the windshield
of a nearby vegetable truck. The truck driver ran out of
a grocery store and cursed, tossing several tomatoes
from the back of his truck at the speeding car. But the
VW was gone.

No use going after it, Daguerre thought, looking back
down the street at a groggy No Tie. He was the only lead
left now if Daguerre was to find Alex.

No Tie was leaning next to the curb, shaking his
battered head in confusion from the beating Daguerre
had given him. He was quite a distance away from Daguerre, but when he saw the angry reporter charging
after him, he began running desperately toward his
gun.

Daguerre ran too, ignoring his sore legs' desire to
limp, his tired heart's plea to rest. He pushed harder. He
was faster than the heavier man, but the Mexican was
closer. Within a few seconds they were both an equal
distance from the gun.

No Tie ran with his hand out, like a runner in a relay
race. Daguerre ran with his head up, teeth clenched,
arms churning.

The gun lay on the sidewalk between them. Waiting. Indifferent to master and victim alike.

Within seconds it was clear to both men who would reach the gun first. Who would be master and who would be victim.

10

No Tie, his mouth hanging open as he sucked air, stopped abruptly, almost skidding on the sidewalk. Then he pivoted and bolted back in the same direction he'd been running from. A moment later he dashed into a narrow alley.

Daguerre cursed as he ran. Another three seconds and he would have reached the gun and could have stopped the bastard. He forced himself to remember Alex's bleeding face, that infectious laugh, so much like Cara's. Somewhere in those thoughts he was able to pick up a little more speed, make his legs kick a little higher.

He ignored the gun as he ran passed it. No time to stop for it now. To slow down, grab it, and then start again could cost him enough time to allow his quarry to lose himself in some building. But he recognized the gun, the make. It was a Makarov. The same as used by the dead man he was refrigerating back in his hotel room.

Seconds later Daguerre was storming down the same dark alley, dodging spilled garbage cans and dirty children hitting each other with sticks, laughing. When he got to the other end, the burly Mexican was gone.

Damn!

He glanced to the left. The crowds mulled along the street in an undisturbed lump. He swung to the right. The same. Thousands of people, but no one hurrying any more than usual.

"Bastard!" an elderly tourist across the street shouted as he bent over packages that were scattered across the sidewalk. He shook a bony fist at the building behind him and shouted again. Then he muttered beneath his breath, wagged his head angrily and gathered up his spilled goods. His wife held his elbow and tried to calm him.

Daguerre looked at the building where the old man had shaken his fist. Whoever had knocked into him had ducked in there.

The City Market.

Got him, Daguerre nodded, twisting his lips into an expression that no one would mistake for a smile. He started across the street.

The City Market was unique. A large marketplace housed in a single building almost a block large. Inside, a high ceiling arced majestically over the people below like that of a cathedral. Small independent businesses crowded together like the tiny squares of a sieve, sifting all the money out of those who passed through the doors. Almost everything one could possibly want to buy was sold somewhere under this giant roof. Scattered about in no apparent order were leather shops, candy stands, record stores. Butchers, clothing, books, fruit, vegetables. And some things that couldn't be seen. Legally.

And the people. Shoppers, both locals and tourists, waded past each other shoulder to shoulder, hip to hip, bodies intimate like lovers. The locals were busy arguing about prices, the tourists were busy holding handkerchiefs over their noses. Daguerre could understand why. The smell was powerful, numbing. The stifling heat, combined with thick swarms of marauding flies, gave the entire market the scent and feel of a large dying animal rotting in the sun. Daguerre had smelled worse things, but not often.

Ten seconds later he spotted his man. No Tie was hunched down, as if he were trying to shorten himself by retracting his head into his neck. He was walking slowly among the crowd, toward the exit, pretending not to be in a hurry. But he gave himself away like most amateurs, and even some professionals. He looked back.

And when he did, he found himself staring across the churning crowd into the burning eyes of Daguerre. It was as if there were suddenly no other people in the building. Only himself and this demonic pursuer who never gave up. Only himself and Daguerre.

No Tie panicked. He stumbled forward, knocking people out of the way as he pushed through the crowd, like a swimmer clawing for shore after sighting a shark.

Daguerre moved more gracefully, slipping, dodging, weaving his way quickly toward the man. He apologized to those he jostled, smiled charmingly, but his eyes never left his prey. With each step he cut the distance, and with each cut in distance his jaw became firmer, his muscles tighter, his heart more eager. It felt almost like hunger.

The Mexican glanced back again and his face paled at how close Daguerre was. He knew there was no point in

trying to outrun this man. He would have to fight again.
He looked around frantically for a weapon.

People in the market recognized the man's crazed expression the way animals sense sickness and began to drift away, moving off to the sides as if it were a dance contest. Mothers grabbed their children's squirming hands and pulled them quickly toward an exit. Others huddled to the sides and waited, wanting to watch what would happen.

No Tie pawed desperately through the nearby booths, searching for something, *anything* he could use to kill Daguerre. Finally he found his weapon, a thick heavy baseball bat he grabbed from a small sporting-goods stand that sold mostly Frisbees with Mazatlán decals on them. He gripped the taped handle with both hands and rested it on his shoulder like a batter stepping up to the plate who had to hit a home run or be sent back to the minors forever. Sweat dripped down his forehead into his eyes and burned. He shook his head briskly and stalked toward Daguerre, his lips smiling with cruel confidence.

Daguerre did not break pace. He marched forward, his face a ghostly calm, as if he were merely out for a short stroll. But when he passed an appliance stand, he paused at a table of cheap portable radios, stopping in front of a large AM-FM model with a long aluminum antenna. He telescoped the antenna to its full length, snapped it off and continued forward to meet his adversary. A fat Mexican woman hiding behind the toasters screamed at him about the cost of the radio. "Deluxe model," she scolded. "Expensive."

No Tie didn't wait for Daguerre to reach him. With

the bat poised over his right shoulder, he ran at Daguerre with a wild yell. When he was within striking distance, he swung with all his might. The heavy wood bat whooshed through the stale air, but Daguerre ducked the blow. The bat swung back again, but lower this time. Daguerre jumped backward, knocking over a table of leather wallets. He stumbled to one knee.

Grabbing his chance, No Tie brought his bat straight down, slicing toward Daguerre's head. But Daguerre rolled to the side and the bat merely smashed the edge of the plywood table in a shower of splinters and cheap wallets.

Now it was Daguerre's turn. On his feet again and circling, he flicked his extended antenna at No Tie like a saber, slashing deeply into his thick neck. Blood welled along the wound like a muddy rut in the road. Daguerre flicked the antenna again, this time at his face, and a bloody jagged gash appeared on No Tie's forehead. The Mexican dabbed his fingers against his forehead, saw the sticky blood and let out with another yell. He swung his bat again, this time grazing Daguerre's right shoulder. Daguerre's antenna clattered to the ground and rolled out of reach.

Daguerre's shoulder tingled. An icy numb spot was spreading slowly down his arm. Sensing his advantage, No Tie swung again and Daguerre saw the bat rocketing toward his face.

Daguerre whirled away, running ahead a few yards before ducking into a nearby butcher stand. The butcher and his wife stood back against the neighboring candy stand, their white aprons splattered with old caked blood and fresh moist blood. Hanging on meat hooks around the refrigerated showcase were horse hooves and a goat's head. Lying prone on the butcher block was a headless goat whose stomach had just been cut open. The stomach and intestines were partially scraped out into a bucket under the table. Flies buzzed overhead like a hovering black cloud.

Next to the headless goat, stuck in the wooden table, was a large heavy meat cleaver. And that was what Daguerre lunged for. He sprang around the showcase, his hand stretched out, ready to grab the cleaver as he ran by. But No Tie was too close behind him, and just as Daguerre grabbed for the handle, the bat smashed down on the butcher block, barely missing his fingers. Daguerre kept moving. It was too late to get the weapon now.

But not too late for No Tie. He looked at the meat cleaver and smiled, shifting the bat to his left hand, jerking the cleaver out of the butcher block with his right. Now wielding both weapons he again attacked Daguerre.

Daguerre ducked the swipe of the bat easily, but the sweep of the meat cleaver caught him on the left shoulder. The blow was light and tentative, barely cutting his shirt, but it was hard enough to sting. And slow him down a little.

If he was to survive, Daguerre realized he would have to attack now. He would only have one chance. Another slice from the cleaver or blow from the bat would be the end of him. And Alex.

Suddenly Daguerre slumped forward, his legs buckling, his feet stumbling awkwardly. His eyes rolled slightly and he began to swoon, dropping down to his knees.

No Tie couldn't believe his luck. But neither did he question it. He lurched forward, his bat and cleaver both raised above his head like an attacking Viking warrior, his eyes swollen with the blood lust that some men get before the kill. His lips twisted into a frightening smile that showed all his yellow back teeth.

That's when Daguerre moved.

He rolled backward, tucking his legs against his chest, his hands anchored on the floor behind his head. Then he kicked out. His heels catapulted like battering rams, slamming into the Mexican's knees. There was a loud cracking sound that even No Tie's howling couldn't drown. He dropped both weapons as he toppled backward on shattered kneecaps. Daguerre jumped to his feet and clamped both hands around No Tie's neck, squeezing with all his might. He didn't want to kill him, merely render him unconscious. He would need him to answer questions.

But he underestimated the Mexican's capacity for pain and desire for self-preservation. Despite the injuries, No Tie's hands somehow found their way to Daguerre's throat and now he, too, was squeezing with all his considerable strength. The two men jostled for some leverage as they leaned their weight into each other.

Daguerre's grip began to loosen. He felt the numbness from his wounded shoulder spreading farther down his arm like a cold mist. The strength was going and No Tie knew it, for suddenly his grip was tightening, his teeth glistening saliva.

Daguerre felt the Mexican's thick stubby thumbs pressing against his windpipe, and he tried to tuck his chin even further. But that wouldn't be enough. He'd have to physically overpower this man if he was to survive.

Fat lazy flies buzzed around them, darted into their faces, brushed against their lips. Taunting them like picadors in a bullfight. They gave Daguerre an idea.

Tensing his neck muscles against No Tie's assault, Daguerre peered out of the corners of his eyes and saw the fly-covered carcass of the goat on the butcher block. He began wrestling the Mexican in that direction. One step at a time, pushing and dragging until they were both strangling each other next to the half-butchered goat.

Then Daguerre did the unexpected. He let go.

No Tie looked startled for a moment, suspicious after being suckered last time. But there was no time for thought now, only action. Only killing. He heaved his broad shoulders into his stranglehold, digging his thumbs into Daguerre's windpipe, crushing the cartilage, pressing it closed.

But Daguerre had not given up. He reached around the back of No Tie's head, grabbed a handful of greasy hair and jerked back. At the same time as he yanked No Tie's head back, he snapped his own forehead straight into the Mexican's face. No Tie's nose exploded with a pop. Blood erupted like lava into Daguerre's face.

No Tie's grip weakened.

And that was enough. Daguerre's movements were clean and swift, too swift even for bystanders to describe accurately. He had the Mexican in a hammerlock now and was forcing his bleeding and broken face down into the gutted goat until No Tie's head was completely buried inside the animal's slimy carcass.

No Tie felt his head swimming amid the stinking entrails, his neck becoming entangled in the squishy intestines. He flailed wildly for air, for one more breath. Daguerre gave him none.

No Tie twisted and bucked, kicked and convulsed, but finally the movements became weaker. And then nothing. The body slumped down and Daguerre let it fall, hunks of mashed flesh clogged No Tie's nostrils. The large intestine was wound around his neck like an octopus tentacle, unraveling from the goat's stomach as he collapsed to the ground.

Quickly, so no one could see, Daguerre slipped the wallet out of the dead man's pocket. He snatched a clean apron from a cardboard box under the table and wiped the blood and guts from his own hands and face. Then he took some money from his pocket and threw it on the goat.

"That should pay for damages," he said in Spanish to the butcher.

The butcher nodded slightly, but made no movement toward the money.

Daguerre paid the fat woman for her radio.

"Not enough," she said. "Twenty pesos more. Deluxe model."

He paid and left.

Now that he had killed his only lead to Alex, he had nothing left to go on. Nowhere to look for Alex. No way to track Centaur. Things couldn't be worse, he thought as he quickly melted into the thick crowd outside the City Market.

But when he arrived back at his hotel, he found he was wrong.

Things *were* worse.

11

A man in a crisp brown police uniform intercepted Daguerre as he walked across the lobby of the El Cid.

"Señor Daguerre?"

"Yes."

"You are under arrest."

Daguerre smiled thinly. "What's the charge?"

The policeman looked surprised at being asked a question with such an obvious answer. "Murder, of course."

Daguerre nodded but did not move. It was much too soon for them to have tracked him down over what had happened at the City Market. The only other murder he had recently committed was the man with the mustache, currently reclining on his bathroom floor. But he had left strict orders with Carlos about not letting anyone into his room. So how could they know?

Daguerre turned to look at Carlos, who puttered guiltily behind the desk. Obviously, he had been the one to identify Daguerre for this policeman.

"The maid." Carlos shrugged under Daguerre's stare. "She sometimes doesn't listen to me. Maybe even does the opposite of what I tell her. We used to go around together. Now I go with her younger sister.

You can see why, no, Señor Daguerre? She never listens." Carlos shook his head at the injustice of it all. "Naturally I give your tip back."

Daguerre waved a dismissing hand. "Women can be dangerous, Carlos."

Carlos nodded with vigor. "*Sí, sí*. This is true."

The policeman nodded too, then nudged Daguerre's arm. "This way, *señor*."

It was not in the direction of the exit.

"Where are we going?"

"Your room."

Daguerre lead the way, with the policeman following a few feet to the rear, his hand resting on the pistol that rode his hip. To Daguerre he looked too young to have used it much in the line of duty. That meant he would be particularly nervous. Daguerre walked slowly and made no sudden moves. He didn't want to be shot accidentally.

When they reached his room, the policeman nodded for Daguerre to step back. Not anxious to spook this nervous boy, Daguerre held both hands away from his body and slowly backed up three steps. The policeman knocked twice on the door.

"*Qué?*"

"Gomez and Señor Daguerre."

"Ah, *sí*. Come in, Sergeant. Bring our guest."

Sergeant Gomez held the door open and Daguerre entered his room. A thin wiry man of about thirty, with a thick black mustache similar to the dead man's, was lying on one of the twin beds, his hands clasped behind his head, his feet up on the bed. He was smoking a filter-tipped cigarette that he held clamped between his front teeth. Smoke billowed around his face like low-hanging storm clouds. He stared at the ceiling, ignoring both Sergeant Gomez and Daguerre.

"Nice hotel, the El Cid," he finally said, looking Daguerre in the eyes. "Swanky."

"So I've been told." Daguerre noticed that the man spoke with an American accent rather than Mexican, though he was obviously of Latin descent.

"You like it here?" the man asked.

"The rooms get a little crowded sometimes," Daguerre replied.

"Expensive?"

"Moderate."

The man nodded and swung his legs over the side of the bed. He stood up, stretched, then halfheartedly tried to slap some of the wrinkles out of his baggy white suit. It didn't help. He brushed his mustache hairs away from his lips; they immediately sprang back.

"Did you know that there was a dead man in your bathroom, Señor Daguerre?"

Daguerre walked over to the bathroom, flicked on the light. The mustached man was still there. Shattered glass lay sprinkled around his head like a mosaic halo. His eyes bulged horribly.

Daguerre nodded. "You're right. There is."

The man in the white suit nodded, too. He fished a crushed pack of Camels out of his jacket pocket and offered one to Daguerre. "American," he said.

Daguerre, who rarely smoked and detested that brand, smiled and took one. "Thank you."

"Welcome." The man in the white suit lit the cigarette for Daguerre, waving the smell of the match away from Daguerre's face. "I learned that as a busboy. The sulfur makes it stink. They teach you all those things while you're waiting for a waiter's slot to open up."

"Where?"

The man brushed the sleeve of his suit again and smiled. "The Big Orange, man. Los Angeles. Born and bred."

"You're a long way from home."

"Am I?"

"Excuse me, Lieutenant Castillo," Sergeant Gomez interrupted. "Do you wish me to remain or should I call in for an ambulance?"

"Go call in," Lieutenant Castillo said. "Use the lobby phone."

Sergeant Gomez gave an uncertain look at Daguerre, then backed slowly out of the room, his hands always resting on his gun.

When he'd gone, Daguerre said, "Someday he's liable to shoot his foot off. Or yours."

"Yeah, well, he's still a little tense when it comes to murder. I just hope I'm not the one with him when he finally pulls that thing out of his holster." He took a deep drag of his cigarette. "Now, where was I?"

"Misspent youth in Los Angeles."

"Well, not totally misspent. I did manage to get a college degree from USC and do some time with the LAPD. Thanks to my parents."

"Your parents?"

"Yes. They worked their little wetback fingers to the bones to put me through school. Interesting business. They made labels for designer jeans and sold them to the local sweat shops to sew into their own cheaper jeans. Quite lucrative, really.''

"That probably dimmed Gloria Vanderbilt's smile by a few hundred watts."

Lieutenant Castillo laughed. "Yeah. My folks' work rides more behinds than Johnson's baby powder.''

"Quite a legacy," Daguerre said, stubbing out his half-smoked cigarette in the ashtray on the dresser. His mouth tasted bitter and his throat burned, but he continued to smile charmingly at Lieutenant Castillo. "What made you leave Los Angeles? Sounds like you were doing all right for yourself.''

"Yeah, I was." He took another drag on his Camel, though there was hardly anything left of it. One more puff and he would burn his fingertips. He exhaled the smoke in a long thin stream, then tossed the butt into the ashtray, not bothering to tamp it out. "I think I just got tired of arresting my own people. Not that they didn't deserve it. Some bad mothers, man. It was just, well, I got to feeling like I'd been hired to ride range on them, like a cowboy keeping the herd from straying too close to the main ranch house where the rich owner's family lives. You know what I mean?''

Daguerre nodded.

The two men looked at each other for a minute, then Lieutenant Castillo smiled. "So I came back to where my family had emigrated from. Mazatlán. Beautiful place, man. You know what that word means?''

"Place of the deer," Daguerre said.

"Yeah. It's a very ancient language. It's called—"

"Nahuatl.''

Lieutenant Castillo tilted his head at Daguerre. "You do your research, don't you, Mr. Daguerre?"

"I try." Daguerre sat on the bed opposite Lieutenant Castillo. "I don't mean to sound unsociable, Lieutenant. I mean, I enjoyed your life story quite a bit. Fascinating, actually. But I'm a bit puzzled. What's all that have to do with the dead man blocking my toilet?"

"Nothing that I can think of. I was just being polite, giving you time."

"Time for what?"

"Time to get your story straight. I know it's going to be a good one. Hell, I've been looking forward to it, like a *Star Wars* sequel. I just wanted you to have a chance to work out all the details in your head before you told me."

"Very considerate of you."

"Well, professional courtesy and all that. I once wanted to be a journalist."

"Yeah? What stopped you?"

Lieutenant Castillo shrugged. "I have trouble with complete sentences. Dangling modifiers. That sort of thing. Four years at USC and I still don't know what 'subjunctive' means. Something to do with leather, I think."

Daguerre laughed.

"Are you ready to give me your statement?"

"Yes."

"I assume it will be truthful. You know we will find out the truth anyway." His face hardened suddenly, the way a policeman's can. "Our jails are really terrible down here, man. The pits."

Daguerre acknowledged the threat and started in with his story. Most of it was the truth. To a point. He realized that Lieutenant Castillo had indeed given him enough time to fabricate a story because those were the easiest to unravel. The more time you have, the more you make up. The more you make up, the easier it is to trip up. Daguerre avoided the trap. He told about the parachute ride, the murdered cousins on the boat, his struggle with the mustached man in the bathroom. But he said nothing of Hannibal S. Kydd, or Centaur, or his fight at the City Market. Or of Alex's kidnapping.

When Daguerre was finished, Lieutenant Castillo offered him another Camel cigarette. Daguerre refused this one. Even charm had its limits. Lieutenant Castillo lit up and blew another thin stream of smoke toward the ceiling.

"Why didn't you phone the police immediately, Mr. Daguerre? Where did you go?"

Daguerre grinned, looked a little ashamed. "I'm sorry, Lieutenant, but I *am* a reporter. And this seemed like such a good story. I knew if I called you guys first I'd be tied up for hours maybe. Meanwhile, another reporter gets tipped and writes the story ahead of me." He threw up his hands in surrender. "I was just doing my job. Like you."

"Of course," Lieutenant Castillo smiled, though he did not looked convinced. "I understand. By the way, the bodies of the two boatmen, Jesus and Fernando, washed up shortly after your little adventure on the beach. We wondered who the tall tourist described by the crowd was. So many different descriptions, they even had you half a dozen different nationalities. Although the ladies all seemed to agree on one adjective: handsome. Or was it 'hunk'? Anyway, one young lady was even more specific. 'Cute buns,' I think was the way she put it.'' His smile broadened. He stood up abruptly. ''This whole thing is a damned nuisance, Mr. Daguerre. This kind of shit can hurt tourism, and that's Mazatlán's main industry. I will look into this killing personally. Meantime, you wouldn't have any theory as to why you were attacked and your room searched, would you?''

''None. Unless it was mistaken identity. Or an attack against something I once wrote. But that seems unlikely.''

''Yes, it does.'' He brushed the sleeve of his jacket again. It seemed to add a few more wrinkles. ''It couldn't have anything to do with the story you're currently working on, could it?''

Daguerre shook his head. ''I'm just doing a travel piece, Lieutenant. For tourists.''

''Maybe you gave an unfavorable review to one of our local restaurants? Insulted a touchy chef?''

Daguerre laughed. ''Maybe.''

''Well, we'll find out. Perhaps you'd like to grab a bite to eat while we finish up here. It'll take a while until we're done. Photographs, fingerprints, the whole routine. We work a little slower here than in L.A., but the results are just as good.''

Daguerre looked at his watch. ''Maybe I will go out and have something to eat, Lieutenant.''

''Good idea. Try El Shrimp Bucket. Very moderately priced. Eleven Olas Atlas, in La Siesta Hotel. Good atmosphere and excellent food.''

"I'll try it, thanks." Daguerre started for the door.

"Oh, Mr. Daguerre?"

"Yeah?"

"You might want to change your shirt first. You seem to have gotten some blood on it."

12

The man called Centaur sat in the balcony of the movie theater, folding a dried apricot in half and poking it into his small mouth with one finger. Except for a slight flexing of the jaw muscles, anyone observing him then wouldn't even know he was chewing, that inside his mouth, tiny sharp teeth were ripping and mashing. Like everything Centaur did, it was over before anyone knew what had happened. Beneath the surface calm, churning activity.

"I am disappointed, Pedro," he said, his voice barely audible so Pedro had to nervously lean closer to hear him. Centaur folded another dry apricot and shoved it between his lips, all the while his eyes fixed on the screen.

It was a bargain matinee of two John Wayne classics, *McLintock* and *She Wore a Yellow Ribbon*, that the theater was showing in hopes of luring a family audience during the hot summer afternoons. If the audience today was any indication, the plan was not working. In the balcony sat only four people: Centaur and Pedro in the front row, and a young couple about sixteen in the back row, too busy groping in each other's clothing to notice either this conversation or the movies. Down below, only five people sat scattered about the entire auditorium, as if afraid to sit too close to anyone else who might be lonely enough to come on a weekday afternoon all alone.

The theater's air conditioner worked only sporadically, and though Pedro had just arrived, he already had a thick film of sweat across his forehead. He wiped it with the back of his sleeve. The dank smell of rotting candy bars and ancient buttered popcorn made his stomach growl, but he said nothing. Right now he was more concerned with the man next to him folding dried apricots .

He tried to explain. "There was nothing I could do, I—"

"Shh," Centaur said. "This is the good part."

They watched the screen silently for a few minutes while John Wayne fought a hundred other men in the middle of a big mud puddle. Behind them, the young girl moaned.

When the scene was over, Centaur turned his head to look Pedro in the eyes. The dark eyes glared like polished stones. But even worse was the pale scar that splashed across his forehead like a blazing comet. The flickering light from the projector seemed to highlight the strange bumps and curves of the scar, almost making it spark. Pedro swallowed something bitter in his mouth.

"You have disappointed me, Pedro." The voice was not quite a whisper.

"Unforeseen complications, sir," Pedro explained, his own voice rising to compensate for his boss's low volume.

Centaur turned back to face the screen. "No excuses, my friend. It only makes matters worse. This man, Daguerre, he is still alive, still free?"

"Temporarily. We do have the girl, the one who was with him. The one taking photographs."

"But Daguerre is still loose, able to investigate, threaten our operation?"

Pedro hesitated. "Yes."

"And who sent this punk, this incompetent to kill him?"

"I did, sir. But Cortez Duran has done work for us before. He has always killed swiftly and without a trace."

Centaur laughed. "But this time he not only fails to eliminate the target, but he litters the area with two extra bodies and then gets himself killed. How can that happen?" He folded another apricot and popped it into his mouth.

"This Daguerre is much more formidable than we realized at first. I have since received a report on him that indicates a man highly skilled in combat." He had not expected this from a simple reporter. "In fact, he has a reputation for sometimes getting rough."

"So do we, Pedro. So do we."

"Yes, sir."

"Why didn't you get this report before you sent this idiot Duran?"

"I didn't think Daguerre would be a problem. It seemed like a simple execution."

Centaur shook his head. In the half-light his face looked delicate, almost girlish. "That was sloppy, Pedro. And your sloppiness has put our whole operation in jeopardy. I have personally planned this entire event, Pedro. Within days our cause shall be millions of dollars richer and at the same time we will have struck a blow right at the heart of the complacent Americans. While we are off counting our money, they will be busy trying to piece together the mangled bodies of the dead women and children we will have left behind.'' He paused, laughed at something Maureen O'Hara said, then continued. ''But you have threatened that by acting hastily and, worse, incompetently.''

''I am sorry, sir. I will do better next time.''

''Perhaps, but how can I be sure?''

The sweat on Pedro's forehead dripped thickly down his brow. He swallowed dryly. ''I swear.''

''Not enough, my friend. I think a little punishment is in order, don't you. Something to remind you of your error. Indeed, a permanent reminder.''

Pedro started to speak, but nothing came out.

Centaur reached into his pocket, fished out a small silver pocket knife. Slowly he peeled open the single blade, all the time watching the screen.

''I would certainly be a poor leader if I did not discipline my own troops. Is that not true, Pedro.''

Pedro nodded.

''But how? That is always the question. What is too much punishment, what is too little? A nagging problem, eh?'' He turned and smiled at Pedro, the tiny feminine teeth shining as white as the scar across his forehead. Reaching out with his free hand, he pinched Pedro's left ear between his fingers. He tugged sharply, laying the edge of the knife behind the ear. ''Perhaps I should cut your ear off. Maybe then you will remember to pay better attention.'' He pressed the knife blade against the soft flesh. Pedro felt the cold blade cutting into his skin.

Centaur pulled the knife away. "But that would be too much punishment, no?"

Pedro sagged with relief.

"Oooh, Tim," the young girl in the back sighed.

Centaur folded another apricot. "Which finger, Pedro?"

"Pardon?"

"Which finger did you use to dial that slob Duran?"

Pedro felt something clawing in his chest. His bowels felt weak, explosive.

"Which finger, Pedro?"

Pedro held up his right index finger.

Centaur tapped the wooden armrest between them. "Put it here."

Pedro laid his finger on the armrest. It quivered there. Crazily he considered struggling, trying to run. But he immediately realized the futility of such a thing. He could never overpower Centaur. He had seen him subdue men twice his size with only a few simple moves. Had seen him once break the neck of a man he was interrogating, leaving the man alive, but paralyzed, unable to move. Then he'd watched Centaur set the room on fire. They'd heard the man's screams all the way down the street as they had driven away.

"So this is the finger that threatens my operation, that almost cost us millions of dollars." He laid the edge of the knife on the first knuckle at the tip of the finger. "Perhaps here?"

Pedro wisely said nothing.

"Or here?" He moved the knife down to the middle knuckle. "Maybe this is enough. What do you think, Pedro? Answer me."

"Well, sir, I—"

Suddenly Centaur moved the knife to the base of the finger where it joined the hand. With a surge of pressure he leaned on the blade and chopped it through the entire finger.

"*Aayyyeee!*" Pedro hollered, though he tried to muffle his scream.

Behind them the young boy shouted, "Hold it down, faggots."

Pedro's finger rolled off the edge of the armrest, plopping onto the concrete floor. It rolled another foot before finally getting caught in a sticky puddle of a melted ice-cream sandwich. He couldn't decide whether or not to pick it up. What would he do with it now? Still, it seemed disrespectful to just leave it there.

Centaur wiped his blade on Pedro's sleeve, handed him a napkin. "Here, you are bleeding all over."

Pedro pressed the napkin against the stub, felt the protruding bone at the center. He felt faint, yet struggled to keep conscious. It would not be wise to make Centaur any angrier. Who knew what he might cut off next?

"Now, we are friends again, eh, Pedro? And now you will do your job. I want the girl killed and I want that reporter, Daguerre, killed. No mistakes. No excuses. Dead. Today." He turned back to the movie, reached into the cellophane bag for another apricot. "Now go."

Pedro forced himself to his feet, still pressing the blood-soaked napkin against his wound.

Centaur held up a dried apricot. "This looks so much like your ear, Pedro, that is why I couldn't cut it off." Then he pushed it into his mouth and laughed. The laugh followed Pedro out of the theater.

13

Daguerre stood in front of the Maya Agencia de Viajes and peered into the large window. Inside it was dark and empty. No grizzled man, no burly kidnappers.

Nothing.

He stepped back from the window and brushed the grime from his hands where they'd pressed against the dirty glass. It had been a little less than three hours since he'd gone through that door, chased a kidnapper in a green VW bug and killed a man in a crowded market-place. But people moved up and down the street as if it had never happened. Indeed, for most of them it never had. Were he to walk into the City Market right now, he would probably find the butcher and his wife busily carving the carcass of that same goat.

The antenna he'd used on No Tie would probably be taped back onto the "deluxe" AM-FM radio, and the radio would be for sale at a slightly reduced price. People would be bargaining, gossiping and buying. Everything would seem to be the same.

But everything was not the same.

Four men were dead. And Alex was missing.

And now the police were involved. Lieutenant Castillo had been amusing and charming by turns, but under-neath the wrinkled white suit he was still all business, all cop. Daguerre knew professionals, and Castillo was the dangerous kind—dangerous to those he was after. It wouldn't take him long to match the descriptions of the foreigner who killed a Mexican in the City Market with Daguerre.

So, if Daguerre was going to stay out of jail and rescue Alex, he would have to move fast. Now. But in which direction? He'd already phoned Alex's father, but Hannibal S. Kydd had checked out of his hotel and flown back to Washington within an hour of their meeting. There was no point in bringing him back again. By the time he arrived, it would be too late. Besides, his kind of help would probably only make things worse.

Daguerre walked across the Avenida Aquiles and wedged himself as inconspicuously as possible between the bank and a religious-book store. For now he would wait. And think.

Things had not been going well so far. Both of his leads were dead. Inexcusable. But considering the circumstances, he had been lucky to come out alive, let alone with a talkative hostage. Still, it had been a little sloppy. And sloppy was not his style.

Daguerre grinned, remembering something his father used to say. His father had been a military man all his life, dedicating almost every waking hour to the service. Aside from his family and the army, Colonel Charles Daguerre had only one other passion: carpentry. Unfortunately he was the worst carpenter in either France or Oklahoma. His shelves were always crooked, his tables always rocked, his doors always stuck. What was worse, young Christian seemed to have a natural knack for building, spending much of his youth repairing whatever his father built.

One day after hammering the last nail into the fence he'd just built around his wife's vegetable garden, Charles Daguerre had stood back with his arm around Christian's shoulder to view the finished project. But even he could see that the fence was already sagging; several boards were split and needed more nails. He'd trampled half the garden building it, yet one slight breeze and it would all crumble into the zucchini. Christian had expected his father to be angry or disappointed, but instead Colonel Daguerre had turned to his son and smiled proudly saying, "I know it is not a work of beauty, my boy. But there is something to be said for *done*."

Daguerre nodded at the memory as he stared into the dark windows of the travel agency. He would be glad when this whole thing was *done*.

No Tie's wallet had not yielded any useful information. A driver's license with the name Luis Valdez of Mexico City. Some papers. A hundred twenty pesos. A dark wrinkled photograph of an unsmiling old woman, probably No Tie's mother.

The gun that Valdez had dropped on the street was also gone, though Daguerre had not really expected to find it. By now it had probably changed ownership five times. Within a week someone somewhere would be dead and the gun would be lying at the bottom of a deep river.

And Lieutenant Castillo now had the mustached man's gun. So Daguerre wouldn't be able to use that as any kind of clue. He'd have to think of something else.

He could trace the owners of the travel agency, or at

least the local manager. Track him down to his home and force him to talk. And talk he would. Daguerre knew how to make him. But if they'd closed down the place, chances were that everyone had gone into hiding by now.

If only he hadn't run into Alex down here everything would have been fine. He could have forced the old man or the two burly thugs to talk. Make them tell what was going on. Where Centaur was.

Daguerre stirred. Something was happening across the street.

A tall American in powder-blue slacks and a Ralph Lauren polo shirt was peering into the window of the Maya Agencia de Viajes, his face pressed against the glass as Daguerre's had been twenty minutes earlier. He was about forty years old, and expensively dressed, right down to the soft leather Bally shoes. A few feet away a woman of about thirty-five stood in a simple but equally expensive blue shift and waited nervously. She kept looking around, fidgeting with her clutch purse, bowing her head when people passed by.

The man knocked sharply on the glass, waited for an answer, then ran up the few steps to the door and knocked again. No one came.

He said something over his shoulder to the woman, then knocked again. This time harder and longer. Still no one came. He walked down the stairs to her and she brushed the smudge from his nose where it had pressed against the dirty glass. The dirt seemed stubborn because she had to wet a handkerchief and scrub the end of his nose with it.

Both of them looked distraught. And nervous.

Daguerre wondered why. Why would a couple who were obviously well-off come to this agency for anything? Especially wealthy Americans who had a particular fetish about clean well-lit offices. And why were they so upset?

Daguerre decided to find out.

The well-dressed couple reluctantly wandered down the street, looking back over their shoulders at the travel agency. When they'd rounded the corner, Daguerre slipped across the street and began following them. This was one lead he was determined to make talk. Whatever it took.

14

"What the hell do you think you're doing?" the man hollered with a mixture of fear and outrage.

Daguerre closed the door behind him and leaned against it, his arms crossed, his face an unsmiling cliff. "I have a few questions, Mr. St. Clair."

"Like hell, mister!" St. Clair spun around and pointed at the phone. "Get the hell out of here right now or I'll call the police."

Daguerre did not move.

St. Clair spoke to his wife without taking his eyes off Daguerre. "Honey, call the police. I'll hold him off."

Mrs. St. Clair moved slowly toward the phone, her voice quavering. "Please, we don't want any trouble. Just go."

"Call the fucking police!" St. Clair barked. He squared his shoulders.

Daguerre smiled and said softly, "The number is 1-3919."

St. Clair gave Daguerre a puzzled look. "What the hell...."

"I'm just here to ask you a few questions, Mr. and Mrs. St. Clair."

"What about?"

"About the Maya Agencia de Viajes."

Mrs. St. Clair dropped the receiver. It bounced off the phone and clattered to the floor. "Bill—"

St. Clair quickly interrupted. "Look, buddy, I don't know who you are or what this Maya whatsis is. We're just down here on vacation. We don't want any trouble from you, and we don't want to spend half a day in the goddamn police station filling out forms just to put you in jail. It's worth a couple hundred bucks to me just to avoid that. And seeing how you're a fellow American—"

"Half American," Daguerre said. "And half French."

St. Clair shrugged. "Same difference." He took out his wallet and began removing money. He counted out three hundred dollars; there was still plenty left over. He held it out to Daguerre. "Here."

Daguerre sighed and walked toward him. St. Clair involuntarily jumped back a step. Then ashamed of his flinching, took half a step forward.

"Put your money away, St. Clair," Daguerre said. "I spent more than that in bribes just to sneak into this place and get your names."

"You what? Impossible. Not this place!"

Daguerre grinned. "I'm here, aren't I?"

Daguerre understood St. Clair's surprise. The Balboa Club de Mazatlán was one of the plushest, most exclusive clubs anywhere. It was a private residential club, extending guest cards only to those recommended by current members or, on a very limited basis, to members of other recognized private clubs. Situated on its own beach just north of the Playa Mazatlán, the club consisted of fifteen individual two-story villas with a total of twenty-two suites and forty rooms surrounding a garden courtyard. It had everything, including a pool, a putting green, and even its own private duck-hunting preserves. Very exclusive. Very private.

But as any reporter worth anything soon finds out, a little lie with a lot of cash opens many doors. So he was here. In Mr. and Mrs. St. Clair's suite. And he wanted answers.

"I want to know what you were doing at the Maya Agencia de Viajes this afternoon. And please don't lie, I'm in a hurry."

That's when William St. Clair made his first mistake.

It was a flurry of kicks. First a side kick, then a roundhouse, followed by a reverse hook kick. Each was executed with classroom perfection, a model of form. There was just one problem. They all missed.

Daguerre dodged or blocked each easily. "Please, Mr. St. Clair," he warned, "this could be dangerous. I only want to talk."

"Dangerous for you maybe," St. Clair growled. "I've been taking *jeet kune do* lessons for five years. That's Bruce Lee's style, you know." Then he launched into another series of shin kicks, each falling short by several inches.

"I'm sorry," Daguerre said sadly, "but I just don't have the time...." And just as St. Clair's leg snapped toward his groin, he stepped to the side and executed a hammer blow to St. Clair's knee. St. Clair gulped with pain, but tried to hit Daguerre's face with a long-range finger jab. Daguerre stepped to the left and delivered a corkscrew right-cross. St. Clair fell backward over a sofa and sprawled into the coffee table.

"Bill!" Mrs. St. Clair screamed and ran to him.

St. Clair hoisted himself onto his elbows and rubbed his jaw. "You know *jeet kune do*?"

"A little. I did a story on Bruce Lee once."

"You're a reporter?"

"Usually. But what I want to know now is not for a story. Not yet, anyway. In any event, your names will never be used. Right now I'm just trying to save a young girl's life. And I need your help."

The St. Clairs exchanged glances. It didn't take long to explain everything.

"We got their name from a friend of ours," Mrs. St. Clair said, handing a fresh bag of ice to her husband.

He pressed it against his jaw where Daguerre had punched him, wincing slightly as it made contact. "Shit, that hurts. Yes, well, we have a home in Beverly Hills. Charing Cross Road. Nothing too fancy, but it's pretty big. But let me tell you something, Mr. Daguerre, I earned every brick in that damn place. I won't go into jokes about how poor my family was, but it was poor enough. I put myself through law school, and now I run a practice that deals exclusively with divorce. Alimony, palimony, you name it. It gets kind of hairy sometimes but—"

"It's a dirty job but somebody's got to do it?"

"Right." He looked at his wife; she smiled weakly. "Anyway, I'm pretty busy with my practice and Sally here has her charities and tennis lessons to keep her occupied. So we needed some help around the house. Maids, gardeners, that sort of thing. We kept hiring people, but none of them really worked out well. They'd want more money, or they wouldn't do the work right. Usually both." He handed the ice pack to Sally and she disappeared into the kitchen. "Well, we aren't the only ones with that problem. Lots of our friends were complaining, too. It got to be the main topic of conversation at parties." Sally returned with a fresh ice bag and handed it to him. "Thanks, babe."

"Another drink, Mr. Daguerre?" she asked.

"No, thank you."

She settled back quietly into her chair.

"Anyway," St. Clair continued, "we were at this party a couple of months ago and we heard from our friends how they solved their help problem. They'd heard about it from friends who'd heard about it from friends ad infinitum. What they do is, they go on vacation in Mexico to Mexico City, Cancun, Puerta Vallarta, Tijuana, Acapulco or Guadalajara. You look up this travel agency, the, uh—"

"Maya Agencia de Viajes," Daguerre offered.

"Yeah, that's it. And you make, um, arrangements with them about what kind of help you need and how many. Then they arrange to smuggle the right people to you. Simple really. And cheaper in the long run. I know of a couple of people who have done that."

"Through this same agency?"

St. Clair nodded.

Daguerre finished his drink and stood up. He nodded to Mrs. St. Clair. "Thank you for your gracious hospitality, Mrs. St. Clair. It was a pleasure to meet you." She smiled politely at him. He turned to St. Clair, who was still reclining on the sofa. He did not offer to shake hands. "Thank you for the information, Mr. St. Clair. You've been most helpful."

"My name better not appear in any article, Daguerre," he said. "Or I'll sue the shit out of you and your bosses."

"I'll pass your message along to Mr. Kydd." Dagger smiled.

"Who?"

"Mr. Kydd. My boss."

St. Clair squirmed nervously. "You mean Hannibal S. Kydd?"

"The one and only. He likes to know when someone threatens him. Gives him a chance to play poker with his staff of lawyers."

"Well, I, uh, didn't really, um, threaten," St. Clair stuttered. "I mean. . . ." He just stood there looking limp and helpless. Captain Kydd's lawyers had ended the careers of a lot of attorneys foolish enough to press nuisance suits on his empire. He never settled out of court, never gave an inch and never forgave people who tried to take advantage of him.

"We'll look forward to hearing from you," Dagger said and walked out the door. Fun was over. As St. Clair closed the door behind him, Daguerre knew what his next step was in saving Alex's life.

Simple, really.

He would just have to get arrested.

15

Lieutenant Castillo paced around his tiny office, a Camel filter-tipped cigarette riding his lower lip, and swatted a rolled-up *Newsweek* magazine against his right leg. He no longer wore his wrinkled white jacket, but his blue cotton shirt was even more wrinkled. Large dark sweat stains formed wet crescents under each arm. He swatted his leg once more, then tossed the *Newsweek* onto his messy desk, where it knocked over a pencil holder and a box of paper clips. He began counting on his fingers.

"First, we have murder." He raised a thumb.

"Self-defense," Daguerre said.

"Next we have assault."

"Self-defense. He tried to kick me."

"Forced entry." Another finger. "You forced your way into their hotel."

"They won't press charges. Besides, you'd never have known about them if I hadn't told you."

"You *haven't* told me!" Lieutenant Castillo shouted. "What are their names?"

Daguerre shook his head. "Can't tell you."

"Okay, okay. How about the murder at the City Market?"

"Self-def—"

"Of course, self-defense." Lieutenant Castillo threw up his hands. "Apparently, Mr. Daguerre, you are the most persecuted man we've ever had in our sleepy little village."

"I wouldn't call 255,000 people exactly a village, Lieutenant."

Lieutenant Castillo grinned. "I forgot. You do your homework." He stopped pacing and stood directly in front of Daguerre, who sat in a small wooden chair next to the lieutenant's desk. The chair was designed for maximum discomfort, but Daguerre sat in it posed and relaxed as if it had been specifically made for him. A stranger entering the room would think it was Daguerre's office rather than Lieutenant Castillo's.

"Tell me something, Daguerre," Lieutenant Castillo said. "You must have known we'd connect you with the City Market killing sooner or later, right?"

"Yes."

"Then why the hell did you walk into this police station and ask for me? You must've known you'd be arrested within seconds. You don't strike me as the guilt-ridden confessional type. And you certainly don't seem suicidal."

"I'm not."

"Then what's your story?"

"I need your help."

Lieutenant Castillo sighed and collapsed into his chair. "This had better be good, man."

Daguerre told him everything. The whole truth. About the Maya Agencia de Viajes. About Hannibal S. Kydd. About the St. Clairs, though he still would not reveal their names. About Alex. About Centaur. When

1. How do you rate _____ ?
   (Please print book TITLE)

   1.6 ☐ excellent   .4 ☐ good   .2 ☐ not so good
   .5 ☐ very good   .3 ☐ fair   .1 ☐ poor

2. How likely are you to purchase another book in this series?
   2.1 ☐ definitely would purchase   .3 ☐ probably would not purchase
   .2 ☐ probably would purchase   .4 ☐ definitely would not purchase

3. How do you compare this book with similar books you usually read?
   3.1 ☐ far better than others   .4 ☐ not as good
   .2 ☐ better than others   .5 ☐ definitely not as good
   .3 ☐ about the same

4. Have you any additional comments about this book?
   _____ (4)
   _____ (6)

5. How did you *first* become aware of this book?
   8. ☐ read other books in series   11. ☐ friend's recommendation
   9. ☐ in-store display   12. ☐ ad inside other books
   10. ☐ TV, radio or magazine ad   13. ☐ other _____
                                             (please specify)

6. What *most* prompted you to buy this book?
   14. ☐ read other books in series   17. ☐ title   20. ☐ story outline on back
   15. ☐ friend's recommendation   18. ☐ author   21. ☐ read a few pages
   16. ☐ picture on cover   19. ☐ advertising 22. ☐ other _____
                                                              (please specify)

   N 12

7. What type(s) of paperback fiction have you purchased in the past
   3 months? Approximately how many?

	No. purchased		No. purchased
☐ contemporary romance	(23) ____	☐ espionage	(37) ____
☐ historical romance	(25) ____	☐ western	(39) ____
☐ gothic romance	(27) ____	☐ contemporary novels	(41) ____
☐ romantic suspense	(29) ____	☐ historical novels	(43) ____
☐ mystery	(31) ____	☐ science fiction/fantasy	(45) ____
☐ private eye	(33) ____	☐ occult	(47) ____
☐ action/adventure	(35) ____	☐ other	(49) ____

8. Have you purchased any books from any of these series in the past
   3 months? Approximately how many?

	No. purchased		No. purchased
☐ Mack Bolan (The Executioner)	(51) ____	☐ Phoenix Force	(55) ____
☐ Able Team	(53) ____	☐ Other Adventure series	(57) ____

9. On which date was this book purchased? (59) _____

10. Please indicate your age group and sex.
    61.1 ☐ Male   62.1 ☐ under 15   .3 ☐ 25-34   .5 ☐ 50-64
    .2 ☐ Female   .2 ☐ 15-24   .4 ☐ 35-49   .6 ☐ 65 or older

Thank you for completing and returning this questionnaire.

PRINTED IN CANADA

NAME _____
(Please Print)

ADDRESS _____

CITY _____

ZIP CODE _____

BUSINESS REPLY MAIL

FIRST CLASS   PERMIT NO. 70   TEMPE, AZ.

POSTAGE WILL BE PAID BY ADDRESSEE

NATIONAL READER SURVEYS

1440 SOUTH PRIEST DRIVE
TEMPE, AZ   85266

NO POSTAGE
STAMP
NECESSARY
IF MAILED
IN THE
UNITED STATES

he was finished, he sat back in his chair and waited.

Lieutenant Castillo took a drag from his Camel, stubbed it out and lit another one. He began sweeping the spilled paper clips back into their tattered box. "Shit, man. Shit. You know?"

Daguerre nodded.

"So you say this travel agency is really a front to smuggle illegal aliens into the States?"

"Yes."

He shook his head. "Clever sons of bitches. But what does this terrorist, uh...."

"Centaur."

"Yeah, Centaur. What's the PLO have to do with illegal aliens?"

"I don't know yet. But they think I know. Or are afraid I'll find out."

"Thanks to your buddy Hannibal S. Kydd."

Daguerre shrugged. "He does what he thinks is right. He's a hard case, but basically decent."

"If you say so." Lieutenant Castillo stubbed out his cigarette and lit yet another. "Clever little bastards."

"Yeah. And when Alex snapped my photo in front of their office, they must have thought she was working on the story with me. That's why they kidnapped her."

"What do you think they'll do to her?"

"Kill her. At least."

Lieutenant Castillo nodded grimly. "Yeah, at least. But why did you come to me? I'd have hit up her old man. He's got the juice."

"Not for what I need."

"And what's that?"

"I need your help in tracking down the kidnappers. I

got the VW's license number, but it's probably for a Mexico City address like his buddy's.''

"Probably."

"If I had the time, I'd cultivate sources and spread some cash around to find them. But there's not enough time for all that. You know the city. You can help.''

"Sure," Lieutenant Castillo said, "I know the city. Better than I know you."

"What's that supposed to mean?"

"It means that so far I have to take your word for a hell of a lot, mister."

Daguerre leveled a cold stare. "It's the truth, Lieutenant."

Lieutenant Castillo returned the stare. "Maybe."

"Look, Castillo, if you're not going to help me...." Daguerre rose to his feet.

"Sit down."

Daguerre remained standing.

"Please."

Daguerre sat.

Lieutenant Castillo pulled an official-looking document out of a drawer. "I've got good news and bad news, Mr. Daguerre. The bad news is that we've traced that gun from the guy in your bathroom."

"Right, the Makarov."

"You familiar with the gun?"

"A little. It's the Soviet equivalent of the Browning."

Lieutenant Castillo grinned. "Research for your travel article?"

"In a way."

"Well, then you also know that it's standard with Soviet-supplied armies."

"It's also made in China," Daguerre added.

"Not this one."

"How do you know?"

Lieutenant Castillo blew smoke through a tiny gap in his two front teeth. It looked like escaping steam. "It's from a cache of weapons the government confiscated in a raid. They were later stolen."

"By whom?"

Lieutenant Castillo wiped his forehead with his sleeve. His lips tightened. "Terrorists."

Daguerre straightened in his chair. "Which group?"

"The JCR—*Junta de Coordinación Revolucionaria*. Are you familiar with this group?"

"Quite familiar. They were established in 1974 as an umbrella group that coordinates the activities of many South American terrorist groups. Like Bolivia's National Liberation Army, Chile's Movement of the Revolutionary Left, Paraguay's National Liberation Front, and Uruguay's Tupamaros. They receive most of their funding from Argentina's *Ejercito Revolucionario del Pueblo*, one of the wealthiest terrorist groups in the world. They also have strong connections with the PLO. The JCR has a powerful headquarters in Paris, from which the assassinations of several South American ambassadors in Europe have taken place. They are ruthless."

Lieutenant Castillo nodded agreement, but his eyes had a quizzical expression. "You are well informed, Mr. Daguerre. An expert, perhaps."

"Just a reporter, Lieutenant."

"Sure. Well, the fact remains that this Makarov is connected with the JCR. Once again I have to ask, what do terrorists have to do with this whole business?"

"I don't know."

"Neither do I, Mr. Daguerre. But I intend to find out."

"In the meantime, let's try to find Alex."

"Yeah, that's the good news. Since we know the dead man's affiliation with the JCR, the remaining kidnapper should be easier to find. We keep quite extensive surveillance on our political groups in this country, you know."

"I know."

"It's funny," he said, "but sometimes I miss those old constitutional rights arguments and all that crap we had to go through to get a wiretap set up. I hated it then, bitched about liberal courts and all that crap like the rest of them. But secretly it made me feel kind of good about the country. Underneath."

Daguerre nodded.

Lieutenant Castillo sighed and handed Daguerre a piece of paper. On it were several typed addresses.

"These addresses are known hideouts of members of the JCR. Of course, there are others we don't know about, I'm sure, but these are quite current."

Daguerre stood up and shook the lieutenant's hand. He understood that Castillo could not become officially involved with this matter yet. It was politically too dangerous. Indeed, he was taking a great risk in both releasing Daguerre and giving him the list of addresses. Either one could destroy his career.

"Thank you, Lieutenant Castillo."

"Good luck, Mr. Daguerre."

As Daguerre walked out of the police station into the cool dusk air, he was already deep in thought, lost somewhere in the thick moist darkness of his mind, where plots and plans were formed, where risks were weighed and success probabilities calculated. When his eyes refocused on the normal world he had walked three blocks.

He permitted himself a small smile. The information Alex's father and Lieutenant Castillo had given him connecting the travel agency with the terrorists made everything clear. Including Centaur's involvement. There was only one explanation. Sure, the agency was a front to smuggle illegal aliens into the United States, into the homes of the wealthy. *But it was also being used to smuggle terrorists, disguised as servants, into the United States.*

But for what purpose?

Daguerre had a plan to find out. But for that he would need Alex. And to rescue Alex he would need a weapon. He glanced at his watch and cursed. He would have to hurry if he was going to get his weapon in time. The toy stores would be closing soon.

16

Daguerre scanned the list once more, checking the items that he'd lined up on the counter of the bathroom in his hotel room. Ring stand, alcohol lamp, 300ml flask, clamps, rubber stoppers, glass tubing, condenser, rubber tubing, clamp holder, collecting bottle, air-trap bottle, 300ml beaker.

He removed the final elements from the large paper bag. Glycerine and sodium bisulfate.

Everything was ready.

He lit the alcohol lamp.

Ordinarily, Daguerre would have preferred a gun when facing the kind of people he was dealing with. But buying one illegally would be difficult considering the small amount of time he had. Locals were suspicious, and in no hurry to deal with foreigners. Everything here took time. Wait and see. *Mañana*.

But Daguerre had to act quickly. Now. And he needed a weapon. So, since he couldn't buy one, he would make one. It had been simple really. Everything he'd needed he'd found in a downtown toy-hobby store. A child's chemistry set and some extra equipment. The proprietor had been happy to unload such slow-moving merchandise. The glass tubing had been covered with dust.

What Daguerre was about to do should have been done outside, for safety's sake, but there was no time to find a safe location. He would take his chances here.

He mixed ten parts of glycerine with two parts of sodium bisulfate in the flask and heated it. Soon the mixture began to froth and he lowered the heat. Gas began to pour from the generating flask through the tubing into the condenser and finally into the collecting bottle. When he noticed the brown residue forming in the tube he shut the heat off. He took several deep breaths, holding the fourth one in. Then he ran to the window and quickly poured the brown residue out into the garden, immediately closing the window. He hurried back to his apparatus and, still holding his breath, plucked the tubing from the collecting bottle and shoved a rubber stopper in.

He stared at the bottle a moment and grinned. Now he was ready. Now he was armed.

17

The first address on Lieutenant Castillo's list was a small bakery on Avenida del Puerto. It was closed, but Daguerre worked the lock easily and searched the entire store. No one was inside, nothing incriminating. On the way out he grabbed a poppyseed roll from one of the tin storage bins and ate while he drove.

The second address was an apartment on Zaragoza in downtown Mazatlán. The building was tall for Mazatlán, the bricks almost black with age and grime. Every window was enclosed in bars or chicken wire. Some even had broken glass spread along the window sill. A fat woman on the third floor pressed her mouth through the bars and yelled down the street for her sons to come home.

Daguerre walked by a few times but decided they wouldn't be stupid enough to keep Alex there. Too many children, old women and old men wandering around the building for anything to be kept a secret for long.

The third address was on Avenida M. Gutierrez Najera, just a little past the railroad tracks. Daguerre had a taxi drop him off a few blocks away from the address.

In his right hand he clutched a plain brown paper bag. Inside the bag was the collecting bottle. He walked slowly, careful not to bump or jar the bag against his leg. If it broke, he wouldn't have time to make more. And without it, Alex did not have a chance.

He spotted the green VW immediately. It had been partially hidden behind some scrawny bushes and other parked cars, but not enough so.

The house itself was really nothing more than a shack, thrown together from all kinds of materials, from adobe to brick to cinder to wood. Whatever the builder could pick up cheap or free.

Inside, voices laughed.

Outside, sat a guard.

Daguerre ducked behind a neighboring house, set the bag down amid the house's modest garden and began inching toward his target.

The guard looked bored. He sat on the dirt stoop and scratched his thick black beard with vigor, occasionally glancing longingly back into the house where the loud voices and laughter were coming from. The older guys had all the fun, all the excitement. He'd joined up for the sake of the Revolution, but that didn't mean he didn't want a piece of ass now and then, too. Especially that one. He sighed and flicked his switchblade into the dry ground at his feet, plucked it out, flicked it again. Same old crap.

Suddenly his head was gripped tightly by unseen arms that kept his mouth from opening, kept him from warning the others. He groped blindly for the knife stuck in the ground at his feet, but his fingers never made it. The hands that were wrapped around his head seemed to push and pull at the same time. The pressure was unbearable. He felt his head quickly snap to the right, heard a dry crack like a distant firecracker. A bolt of pain clawed up his spine, gnawed into his brain. There was a thick soothing warmth. Then darkness.

Daguerre eased the dead man with the broken neck softly to the ground. He grabbed the switchblade, almost identical to the one he'd taken earlier from Duran, and dashed back to the neighbor's garden to retrieve his paper bag. Gently he removed the bottle, tossing the paper bag on the ground. With the bottle in his right hand and the switchblade in his left, he crept up to the window and peered inside.

What he saw made him sick.

Three men sat cross-legged on the floor, drinking beer and laughing. One of them, a gray-haired old man with no teeth, drunkenly waved a gun in the air. A Makarov.

The second man was young and muscular. He wore no shirt, only a series of cheap gold-plated chains. With every movement he made, several lumpy muscles would ripple across his chest and back.

Daguerre recognized the third man as the driver of the green VW bug. The man who'd kidnapped Alex. He was trying to pry open another bottle of beer using the trigger guard of his Makarov. The others laughed at his bumbling.

In the middle of the group, stretched out on the floor, was Alex. Naked.

Daguerre could see the abuse already done. Her lips were swollen and caked with blood. A small black-and-blue knob had risen on her left cheek. Dark finger bruises like chevrons marked her neck and breasts, where they had squeezed too hard. She looked frightened and in pain, but he could see she was struggling not to show it to the men laughing and drooling around her.

Daguerre swallowed something bitter in his mouth.

"We have waited long enough," the old man with no teeth finally said, slamming his bottle on the floor. Beer sloshed onto his hand which he licked off. "I am ready *now*!"

"*Si*," the muscle-bound one agreed. "I, too, am ready, Pablo." He began to rotate his hips in an obscene gesture. The others laughed.

Pablo, the driver, shrugged. "Perhaps you are right. She can tell us nothing more. And I am tired of listening to her insults. We will kill her now."

The old man cackled. "Kill her, yes, Pablo. But first things first." He began to unbuckle his belt.

They all laughed.

"You sure you can get it up, old man?" Alex spat, her voice weak. Defiant only by habit now.

The old man smiled through brown tobacco-stained gums and laid the cold muzzle of his pistol against Alex's soft breast. "We shall see, little one."

Pablo's hand disappeared between Alex's legs and she jerked back. "Yes," he laughed, "we shall *all* see. Maybe even young Juan out there. Eh, Juan?" he called over his shoulder.

The answer he got was not what he'd expected.

Daguerre burst through the door like an Apache warrior, his eyes cool, his lips curled in a frightening visage. The three men were stunned for a few seconds, long enough for Daguerre to smash his bottle against the floor and watch the homemade tear gas mushroom upward in thick ghostly billows.

Then everything was motion.

The old man held up his unbuckled pants with one

hand and aimed his pistol with the other. Daguerre did not give him a chance to steady his aim. He leaped through the rising gas, still holding his breath, and plunged his switchblade into the old man's heart. The old man gasped, let go of his pants and wobbled to the left. His pants dropped around his ankles, tripping him. By the time he hit the floor, he was dead.

Daguerre heard Alex coughing, saw her struggling to pull herself to her feet. But he couldn't stop to help her. There was still one more gun to take care of.

Pablo was shooting now, but the tear gas had blurred his vision and was causing him to cough with such racking spasms that his aim was way off.

"Watch it, Pablo!" Muscles cried. "You almost hit *me*."

"I don't care," Pablo shouted back and squeezed off another round.

There was no time to grope through the tear gas for the old man's gun. Besides, Muscles was starting to move in his direction. Daguerre's knife would have to kill a second time.

"Pablo!" Daguerre shouted and ducked.

Pablo swung around and fired off two more rounds. But by now Daguerre was squatting a few feet in front of him. He waited quietly on his haunches, listening as Pablo shuffled blindly through the smoke, one arm groping, the other pointing the Makarov. When the footsteps were within striking distance, Dagger leaped straight up, his knife thrusting into Pablo's startled body. The knife entered the stomach just below the sternum, but Pablo jerked back so suddenly, the blade snapped free from the handle.

"Cheap knives," Daguerre muttered.

But Pablo didn't hear. He dropped his gun and began frantically tugging at the broken blade still embedded in his chest. But the thin metal was too slippery with blood and his fingers slid off helplessly. Finally Pablo cursed and thudded to the floor.

"Pablo. *Pablo*!" Muscles yelled.

Dead silence.

Daguerre crouched, his fingers curling around Pablo's gun. The smoke was too dense to see clearly, and Muscles wasn't making any noise. He could be anywhere. At least he didn't have a gun, Daguerre thought as he started to rise. Now he had the advantage.

Then he felt thick hard arms clamp around his chest and squeeze. The air he'd been holding in to avoid breathing the tear gas was immediately crushed out of his lungs. The arms tightened. Daguerre could feel his ribs starting to give, felt a sharp pain shoot through his abdomen. He opened his mouth for air, but none came.

Still clutching Pablo's Makarov, Daguerre shifted his weight to allow him to loosen his right arm just enough to shove the gun muzzle against Muscle's cheek.

Muscles felt the cold metal before he saw it. He screamed, *"No!"*

Daguerre pulled the trigger.

The back of Muscles's head exploded in a pink mist of bone, brain and blood. The gold-plated chains around his neck jangled as his body flew backward into the tear gas, twitched a moment, then lay still.

Daguerre shook his head briskly. The gun had thundered close enough to his ear to leave a loud phantom ringing. It was hard to hear Alex's cry of his name.

"Chris...."

Daguerre's eyes were burning now and he started to cough, but he managed to grab Alex under her arm and drag her out of the house. She trembled with a series of hacking coughs.

"Chris...God...I...."

"No time," he said, hopping over the dead guard, Juan. "Help me get his pants off."

She stumbled forward, still coughing. "What for?"

"For you to wear."

People from neighboring houses had begun to pour out from behind their screen doors. They watched dispassionately as Daguerre stripped the dead man of his clothes and as Alex climbed into them to cover her nakedness.

Sirens wailed in the distance. Approaching.

"Let's get moving." Daguerre motioned as she zipped her pants. If they were caught here, even Lieutenant Castillo would be forced to arrest them.

Alex looked back at the house with the tear gas floating out of windows and doors like a thick fog, and at Juan's body with its neck twisted at such an awkward angle. She shook her head. "God, what a mess."

Daguerre grabbed her hand and pulled her into the night. "Maybe," he said as they ran. "But there's something to be said for *done*."

18

Twenty minutes later they checked into the Hotel de Cima with only the slightest of raised eyebrows from the night clerk. Daguerre drew a hot bath for Alex and let her soak by herself for almost forty minutes.

Finally he knocked on the door and asked, "Are you okay in there?"

"Yeah," she said quietly. "Just trying to get clean."

Daguerre went back to his chair. A few minutes later he heard the water gurgling down the drain. The bathroom door opened and Alex stepped out with a towel wrapped around her body and another wrapped around her hair.

"Feel better?"

"Yeah, great," she said a little too cheerfully. "By the way, thanks for saving my life."

"A reporter's work is never done."

"They really were going to kill me, weren't they?"

"Yes."

She shrugged. "That's what I thought. Old Pablo spent a long time on the phone with somebody. When he came back to join the party he said he'd been ordered to kill me. But if I was real nice to him and his friends, maybe he wouldn't."

"What did you say?"

"I told him it wasn't worth the price."

Daguerre smiled. "You're pretty tough, aren't you?"

"Yeah, I'm tough. I'm Captain Kydd's daughter." She sat on the edge of the bed and began toweling her hair dry.

"Did you catch any names while you were there?"

She stopped a moment to think. "Just the names of the guys in the house. And the guy on the phone."

Daguerre leaned forward. "What was his name?"

"Let me think. Uh, something weird. Like Knife Nasal. Something like that."

Daguerre tensed. "Naif Nasil?"

"Yeah, that's it."

"So *that's* Centaur."

"Who?"

"Centaur. A code name, a *new* code name for an old enemy. He used to be called Rabid."

"Cute."

"Yeah, cute. The result of a little habit of his. Biting the tongues off people he killed."

"Jesus," she frowned. "And you know him?"

Daguerre sat back in his chair and exhaled. He didn't notice that he was grinding his teeth. "I know about him. He's pretty high up in the Popular Front for the Liberation of Palestine."

Alex stopped toweling again. "Jesus."

"Yeah."

"But what does a Palestinian terrorist want with me?"

"Nothing. They wanted me."

She jumped up from the bed. "Aha! Then I was right! You are working on a big story. I was right all along."

"No you weren't. Sit down and listen. And don't interrupt." Daguerre explained everything to her. As he did, he watched the color drain from her face.

Alex shook her head slowly. "Shit. I went through all that because of a *mistake*? Not only that, but my own father triggers the whole thing off. Damn."

Dagger leaned over to comfort her, but before he reached her she brightened with another thought. "Hey, this could turn into a lucky break. At least we've still got a *story*!"

"You *are* tough, aren't you?"

"When I have to be." Alex stood up and walked over to him. Daguerre also stood up. Their faces were less than six inches apart. He smelled jasmine mixed with Ivory soap. Her voice was soft and low. "Would you mind, Chris, if I wasn't a tough, plucky broad for about five minutes?"

"I wouldn't mind at all."

And she was in his arms, her face buried against his broad chest, her shoulder heaving with sobs. He felt her tears soaking through his shirt and he held her tighter.

"I'm sorry," she said, pushing away, wiping her eyes with the corner of her towel. "That was more than five minutes."

He smiled and kissed her on the forehead. Then the cheek. Then lightly on the sore lip.

She threw her arms around his neck and pulled her body next to his. Somehow both towels fell away.

He lowered her gently to the bed and for a moment he was reminded of how gently he'd lowered Juan to the ground after snapping his neck. He thought of Cortez Duran, eyes bulging against the cold tile of his bathroom floor; No Tie, his nostrils stuffed tight with goat flesh; Muscles, Pablo and the old man, dead and bleeding in a shack a few miles away. An avalanche of corpses tumbled on top of him. He forced the image out of his mind as Alex rolled on top of him and began tugging his clothes off.

Her hands were firm and eager, exploring his body with tender insistence. Then her lips followed her hands and he felt her tongue flickering over his skin like a moist eel. Finally he felt the warmth of her mouth surround him.

Daguerre's own fingers were moving and within minutes Alex rolled onto her back and whispered, "Please, Chris. Please."

Her hips lifted to meet his, and he could feel the muscles of her thighs locking around his buttocks. The thrashing and moaning increased in speed. Her breath puffed sweetly in his ear. The thin film of sweat on both their bodies made them slippery and he could feel her thighs slipping away.

She pushed harder against him, gasped, pushed, dug her fingers into his arms and back. For a moment, Daguerre could not tell where his body ended and hers began. Nor did he care.

They collapsed together in a warm damp tangle.

"Hold me, Chris," she said. "Just hold me."

He kissed her cheek and held her.

They napped for twenty minutes, finally unraveling themselves. Alex looked well-rested and happy, her old tough self again.

"Well," she said, pulling the sheet over her hips, "now that I know the story you're working on—and don't try to deny you're on this story, regardless of how you got into it—you'll have to take me on as a part-ner.''

''And if I don't?''

''I'll spill my guts to my own paper.''

''That could hurt your father.''

''Maybe, but he's a big boy. I'm not doing anything he wouldn't do.''

''That's true.''

She narrowed her eyes suspiciously. ''Would you care?''

''About what?''

''If the Captain got hurt.''

''Not at all.''

''I think you're lying, Chris. You may hate him for something he did to you once, I don't know. But there's also a part of you that still cares about him. The way he still cares for you.''

Daguerre laughed. ''Considering the mess we're in, he has a funny way of showing it.''

''He didn't know I'd get involved. He had faith in your ability to handle the situation. And I'm betting you want to prove to him he was right.''

''You charge by the hour for this psychological pro-file, or is it part of a package? Want to read my tea leaves, study my life line?''

She looked hurt. ''It's free with every roll in the hay, buster. Along with a little tidbit of news even you don't know.''

''Like what?''

''Like the fact that dad set up a trust fund for your fiancée's younger brother after her death. When he reaches twenty-one, he'll come into enough money for college all the way through a Ph.D. if he wants. You didn't know that, did you?''

''No.''

''No one's supposed to know yet. Except my spy.''

''Your mother.''

''Right.''

Daguerre wished he smoked. It would feel good to have hot smoke swirling through his lungs, burning out the confusion he felt inside. He pictured Hannibal S. Kydd in his black wraparound sunglasses, the scar tissue clumping under the rim of one lens. It was just like the bastard to do something like that. But did he do it out of affection, or because he intended one day to use it as leverage against Daguerre? Either was possible from him.

He remembered the many times Captain Kydd had sat in Daguerre's parents' home in Oklahoma, playing chess with his father, flirting harmlessly with his mother. The three of them talking about Dagger as if all three of them had raised him together.

Daguerre nodded at Alex. ''Okay, okay, you're in.''

''Really? That was easier than I thought.'' She sat straight up in bed. ''What's the catch?''

''Catch?''

''Yeah. You wouldn't give in this easy unless there was something else involved. Something I'm not going to like.''

''Well, there is one thing.''

''I knew it, damn it. What?''

He smiled. ''Why, we get married, of course.''

She stared blankly at him. ''You're kidding?''

Daguerre threw his head back and laughed.

19

"Welcome to Cancún, *señor*...."

"St. Clair," Daguerre said, squeezing Alex's shoulder affectionately. "William and Sally St. Clair."

The clerk glanced at the reservation ledger in front of him and nodded happily. "Of course, Señor St. Clair. We have been expecting you."

"Nice little place you've got here," Daguerre said, imitating the arrogant tone and clipped speech of the real St. Clair. "Quaint."

The clerk, a thin middle-aged man with obvious pride in his work and hotel, pretended not to be shocked at the American's rudeness. Instead he forced a smile onto his lips. "*Sí*, Señor St. Clair, the Cancun Caribe is the nicest hotel in this part of Mexico. Some say in all of Mexico. We are *nine* stories high with 208 rooms. Because we are so situated at the far end of the island spit, we have the most beautiful section of beach."

"Great," Daguerre said.

"Oh, there is more, *señor*," the clerk continued, "Much more."

Daguerre was sorry he'd played his role so well.

"Each room has a balcony with a view of the sea. Of course, all the rooms also have refrigerators and bars. Stocked, naturally."

"Naturally," Daguerre said.

"Naturally," Alex said.

The clerk looked at both of them, trying to decide whether or not to continue the lecture, but was interrupted by an elderly Canadian couple checking in.

Alex tugged on Daguerre's sleeve and whispered, "Don't ham it up too much. Not all Americans are obnoxious, you know."

"This one is."

"Look, before we go out and bust up a gang of international smugglers and terrorists, there's one thing I'd like to do first."

"What's that?"

"Eat! I'm starving. In another hour I'll be nothing but skin and cellulite."

Daguerre chuckled.

The clerk returned, his polite smile pasted back into place, his pride somewhat restored. Daguerre sensed another lecture coming on and quickly said, "My wife and I are anxious to do a little sightseeing first. Please send our luggage up to our room."

"But our rooms are magnificent, *señor*. You should see them first. The view alone—"

Daguerre smiled and waved his way out the door.

Once outside they both laughed.

"Food," Alex mugged, hanging her tongue out panting.

"Okay. How about the Playa Chac Mool. It's a small but extraordinarily charming restaurant complete with glass walls and thatched roof. The food is excellent, at least it was the last time I was there."

"I know you're going to think this is real tacky of me,

Chris, but I've about had my fill of Mexican food. How about Chinese or French?''

"I know just the place. Las Palapas on the central plaza. Terrific Italian food."

"Just what my thighs need, pasta. Let's go."

They were silent through most of the meal, each recalling the events of the past two days and wondering what lay ahead for them.

For Daguerre, convincing the St. Clairs to cooperate with him had been easy. A simple threat had done it. "You will not only give me your letter of introduction for these people, but you will disappear for three days somewhere under a different name," Daguerre had told them. "Or you'll have some explaining to do to both the American and Mexican authorities. I imagine the Bar Association might not be too happy about that."

"You promised not to tell anyone," St. Clair had whined.

"I lied."

Convincing Alex had also been easy. She was anxious to break out of gossip sheets and into real journalism. Daguerre recognized her need to prove her worth to her successful father, and he had allowed that to influence her. Maybe it was the wrong thing to do, considering the danger, but he needed her to complete his cover. And at least she knew about the risks. He couldn't take the chance that someone who'd seen him in Acapulco or Mexico City or Mazatlán might also recognize him here. The gray dye at the temples helped. Changing the part in his hair also made a difference. The rest was attitude. The condescending thrust of his head and his arrogant tone. The stooped walk. And of course Alex at his arm, complete with blond wig, expensive dress and a slight Southern lilt to her accent.

"I can't believe daddy told them you were after them. At least without warning you first."

"He didn't want me to have a chance to refuse."

She sipped her wine and shook her head. "God, that's so typical of him. Captain Kydd. Shoots from the hip and lets the bodies fall where they will."

"Yeah, but he's a hell of a journalist."

"But you quit him."

Daguerre shrugged. "Personality differences. He wanted mine to be just like his."

"I've been there," she nodded, staring deep into his eyes. "How'd you get hooked up with the Captain in the first place?"

"Family tradition, I guess. My mother did some photography for one of his magazines. I remember when I was fifteen she'd done this whole photographic essay of San Francisco for the Captain. Well, she captioned one shot of the city at night describing it as looking like 'the gaudy lining of a pimp's favorite jacket.' Your father had that caption cut and mother stormed around the house for a week afterward threatening to do an exposé of *him*. She quit instead."

"So quitting him is also family tradition?"

"I guess so. Except that he's still close friends with her and my dad."

"Staying friends, that's one family tradition you didn't keep, huh?"

"There were reasons."

They ate silently.

Alex stared off through the restaurant, a sadness in

her eyes that hadn't been there before. Daguerre recognized the look, the mounting realization of what had just happened to her and how close she'd been to death.

"Have you ever been to Cancun before, Alex?" Daguerre asked refilling her wineglass with a good clear Soave.

"Once. I did an article on the Club Med they have down here. What the swinging singles do after dark, that sort of thing."

"And what do they do after dark?"

She grinned wickedly. "Just what you'd expect."

"Hmm. Research must have been stimulating."

She wiggled her eyebrows and giggled. "After all, it was an undercover assignment. But don't worry, it's not nearly as stimulating as this assignment."

Daguerre's face grew grim. "We're not hunting a juicy bit of gossip now, Alex. We're hunting a man, a very dangerous man. Naif Nasil has a reputation."

"What kind of reputation?"

"It depends on who you talk to." He took another sip of wine, swirled it in his mouth a moment, then swallowed. "His enemies see him as a fanatical perverted butcher who likes biting the tongues out of his victims' mouths. And he has a specialty when it comes to victims."

"What specialty?"

"Children mostly."

Alex paled and licked her dry lips. She pushed her half-eaten fettucini away. "Jesus. If that's how his enemies see him, how do his friends see him?"

"The same. Only for a good cause."

Alex looked at the food in front of her and made a face. "What's he do with them?"

"What?"

"The tongues."

"Oh." Daguerre used his fork to spear a few strands of fettucini from Alex's plate. "He forces his recruits to eat them as an initiation. They're an elite group of terrorists. It's considered an honor."

Alex put her hand over her mouth and took a deep breath. Daguerre speared another forkful of her fettucini.

"I just wanted you to know what kind of people we're dealing with. What you could be getting into."

"Thanks a bunch."

Daguerre shrugged. "You wanted in. What's happened so far is nothing compared with what happens next. Within a few minutes you and I are going to walk right into the lion's den. There are no guarantees."

"It'll make one hell of a story, though," she said with false bravado.

"Sure. If we live to write it. Besides, the story won't be complete until we find out why they're smuggling Palestinian terrorists into the United States. What's their plan? And when is it going to take place?"

Alex shook her head while playing with some bread crumbs on the tablecloth. "I don't see how they managed to smuggle them in as Mexicans. You'd think people would notice."

"Not really. The skin color is similar, so are the facial features. Oh, there are distinct differences, but most Americans aren't interested in those differences so they won't notice them. It's rather ingenious, actually."

Alex reached across the table and put her hand over Daguerre's. "This means more than a story to you, doesn't it, Chris?"

Daguerre was silent.

"I know about your fiancée. How she was killed. I overheard dad telling mom a while back. You must have really loved her."

Not loved, but *love*, he thought. It was crazy, he knew, to feel that way about someone who was dead. Yet, deep, deep inside, in a place only Cara had ever reached, Daguerre still burned with love for her—and hate for her murderers.

Daguerre picked up the check and tore off the bottom stub. "Expense account," he explained. Then he threw down enough money for the bill and a generous tip.

"I'm sorry, Chris," Alex said, rising. "I didn't mean to pry."

He gave her a wink and a smile. "Let's go. We've got a lion's den to enter."

20

Cancun's branch of the Maya Agencia de Viajes was remarkably similar to Acapulco's branch and Mazatlán's branch. Perhaps filthier.

It was located on the second floor of a two-story building on Quintana Roo. Nothing outside the rundown building indicated there was a travel agency inside. Only someone who already knew it was there could find it.

Daguerre and Alex entered the office through a splintered door with the agency's name painted sloppily on it. Inside, there was an old wooden table with crosshatches of cigarette burns in it. Behind the table sat a man in his late twenties eating a thick burrito.

"Mr. Blanco?" Daguerre asked.

The man took another bite of his burrito and studied Daguerre from head to foot, calculating from the worth of his clothes, the wearer's annual income. He was usually surprisingly accurate.

"Closed," the man said through his half-chewed mouthful. He held up his dripping burrito. "Lunch."

Daguerre's arm was around Alex's shoulder and he could feel her body quivering slightly. The man behind the table continued munching, never taking his eyes from Daguerre's.

"Your agency was recommended to me," Daguerre said, reaching into his jacket pocket. "By Mr. Sommers of Beverly Hills." The man behind the table jumped to his feet and pointed a gun at Daguerre's chest. A Makarov.

"I have a letter," Daguerre said, trying to sound frightened.

The man dropped his burrito onto the table, wiped his greasy fingers on his jeans and walked toward Daguerre and Alex. When he was less than three feet away he snapped his fingers. "The letter, *señor*."

Daguerre slowly removed the letter of introduction that St. Clair had brought down from the friend who had used these services before. The Mexican shook it open and read. His lips moved slightly as he read.

When he was finished, he nodded twice and smiled. With a friendly wave of his hand he walked back to the table and dropped the Makarov back into the drawer.

"Cancun is a remarkable place," he said. "Did you know that this entire area was once almost completely uninhabited? *Sí*, it is true. This entire resort area was built only after government computers picked this as the most potentially successful resort area in all of Mexico. Computers. Amazing, no?"

"Yes," Daguerre agreed.

The man sat back down behind the table and resumed chewing on his burrito. "Now, Señor St. Clair, just what can Cancun provide for you?"

Daguerre looked at Alex. "What do you think, Sally?"

Alex's voice was quiet and submissive. "Well, a maid would be very nice."

"Yes, yes, a maid," Daguerre agreed. "Someone who's not afraid of a little work."

The man nodded with understanding, like a plastic surgeon listening to a patient describe the kind of nose she always wanted. "A maid," he said.

"Yes, a maid. And we have two small boys, Señor Blanco, who are always into some mischief or other. You know how boys can be."

"*Sí*, I have two sons of my own."

Daguerre doubted that but continued. "As I said, they're always running around or falling somewhere and coming home with a cut or a bloody nose or some such thing. So we'll need someone who's not afraid of a little blood."

The Mexican swallowed his mouthful of burrito and smiled hugely, his teeth flecked with shredded beef. "*Sí*, someone who'd not be afraid of a little blood. I think I have just such a person."

They all smiled at each other.

21

"Are you sure this is the place, Chris?"

Daguerre looked up at the street signs. "The corner of Avenida Revolución and Seventh, in front of the fronton. That's where he said to wait."

Alex sighed. "Okay, but we've been waiting for more than an hour."

"Relax, you've been to Tijuana before."

"Yeah," Alex frowned, looking around the street, "that's why I can't relax."

Daguerre permitted himself a smile. There was something about Tijuana that uneased people. He had been here many times, and always there was the vague feeling of apprehension. A sense that anything could happen— and would. Maybe it was from seeing too many movies, but more likely it was from the many nefarious activities his reporting had uncovered there. And now there was one more. Perhaps the worst of all.

Like most border towns, Tijuana churned with people, noise and smells, blending all three until they were almost indistinguishable. The streets and alleys were packed tight with merchants eager to bargain and argue and curse until giving in for a price that, they complained, would surely mean starvation for their entire family. And there were the tourists, mostly American, happily bargaining for a lower price, but still suspecting they'd paid too much.

It was a city bursting with its 750,000 people, losing its race to modernize despite the many new streets. Shanties and tin houses grew like mutant weeds on the surrounding hillsides, grim landmarks to those only passing through.

The main street, Avenida Revolución, pushed imported Japanese goods to the tourists, many of whom were from San Diego, only seventeen miles north. And Avenida Juarez boiled with cheap mass-produced American goods sold to the locals. In between were the endless tawdry strip joints, clubs, bars and dubious restaurants. Typical of border towns around the world, but not typical of the grand Mexico that Daguerre knew.

Daguerre glanced at his watch. So far they'd followed instructions exactly as Señor Blanco had given them through his mouthfuls of burrito. They had flown into Tijuana airport that morning and taxied immediately to this location. And waited.

"Jesus," Alex whispered to herself at the sight coming down the street toward her. It was a young teenage girl, thin and ragged, carrying a baby on her back, equally thin and ragged. "She can't be much more than fifteen."

The girl shuffled up to them and held out her hand. "*¿Por favor?*"

Alex dug into her purse and pressed a five-dollar bill into the girl's bony hand. The girl tucked the bill away and smiled a toothless grin. Alex tried to smile back but it came out more like a frown.

Daguerre knew what was happening, but said nothing. It would not be part of William St. Clair's character to notice the fat Mexican sidling along the wall, pretending to be looking at the jai-alai posters. Nor was he supposed to notice how long the little beggar girl was lingering, distracting their attention.

Therefore he tried to act surprised when the fat man jabbed him lightly in the side with a long pocket knife. "This way, Señor St. Clair."

The fat man was breathing heavily from the heat and excitement, and Daguerre could smell some kind of fish on his breath. And a hint of cheap beer. He wore a loose safari jacket that did little to conceal his tremendous stomach. A Panama hat was tilted low over his forehead. His mustache was razor-thin above his puffy lips, as if someone had drawn it on with a fine-point pen. He looked at the beggar girl and jerked his head. She nodded and hurried away. The baby bounced happily on her back.

"Let's go, dear," Daguerre nudged Alex.

Alex saw the knife. "Bill!"

"It's okay, Sally," Daguerre said, relieved at how quickly she'd picked up her character. "This gentleman just wants us to go with him."

"*Sí*, Señora St. Clair," the fat man shrugged apologetically at the knife. "This is just a pre...uh, pre—"

"Precaution," Daguerre said.

"*Sí*. Precaution. Thank you."

They walked through several streets and alleys, weaving and winding among the laughing tourists. Three American teenage girls, braless in tight suggestive T-shirts, pointed at Daguerre and giggled, one going so far as to shout, "I love you, hunk." The others giggled some more.

Alex turned around and whispered, "Try to turn down the charm, will you, darling? You're giving the back of my neck a sunburn."

"What?" the fat man asked, moving closer, his hand buried deep in a large pocket of his safari jacket, his chubby fingers wrapped around his knife. "What did she say?"

"She wants to know how much farther."

"Soon," the fat man said. "Soon."

Their speed was impeded slightly by Alex, who had gotten out of the habit of wearing high-heeled shoes years before, and now was having trouble keeping her balance at this pace. Daguerre noticed her problem and clamped a steadying hand under her elbow.

A few minutes later they arrived.

"In there," the fat man said, nodding at the weather-beaten door to an upholstery shop. There was a hand-lettered sign on the door that read, in English, Closed.

Daguerre held the door open for Alex, who stepped through with a nervous smile. Inside the store was empty and dark.

"All the way back," the fat man said, clumsily locking the door behind him.

Daguerre and Alex walked slowly to the back of the store. Behind the green Formica counter was an open doorway covered by a bright piece of cloth hanging down as a partition. Alex stopped in front of the cloth door and looked back hesitantly at their guide.

"Go in," he barked, pointing now with his open

knife. His breathing had become heavier now and the smell of fish and beer more foul.

The three of them went through the door.

The room on the other side was a double garage, though the garage doors were shut. Some light filtered through a dirty window, half of which was broken, with a piece of cardboard taped over the hole. There was a scattering of machinery and tools, all for upholstering. At the far end of the garage, a blue 1969 Thunderbird was parked, its doors all open and the front seats removed.

"Finally, my friends," a tall thin man said pleasantly as he stepped out of the shadows. He was somewhere in his sixties, though he was probably a few years older than he looked. His light cotton suit was similar to Daguerre's, only more expensive. Much more. He sported a white goatee and long white sideburns, like a Spanish patriarch. He was what Daguerre's mother would have called "natty." His father would have been less kind. But between the sleeve of his beige suit and the expensive gold watch on his wrist, Daguerre noticed the tip of a faded tattoo peeking out of the cuff.

"Put that away!" he snapped at the fat man when he saw the knife. "Mr. and Mrs. St. Clair are our guests."

"B-b-but—"

The gray-haired man's eyes flared briefly and the fat man folded his knife and slipped it back into his jacket.

It was a good performance, Daguerre thought, but he'd seen better. It was obvious that the old man was in charge of this phase of the operation, and that it was he who not only arranged for the beggar girl, but who had instructed Fatty to bring them here by knife point. Well, one good performance deserves another.

"I don't know what's going on here," Daguerre shouted. "But I'm not used to being treated in this manner. I'm an attorney, not a thug. Your man and his knife nearly scared my poor wife to death." He hugged Alex to his shoulder, who looked appropriately frightened. "I thought I was dealing with businessmen, not hoods. We don't need a maid or anything else *that* bad that we'd put up with this kind of bullshit."

The gray-haired man stepped forward again, shaking his head in sympathy. "Of course, Mr. St. Clair. I quite understand your feelings. Permit me to introduce myself. I am Hector Martinez." He bowed slightly. "Sometimes in this kind of business it is necessary to take certain unpleasant precautions."

"*Sí*," Fatty said. "Precautions."

Martinez gave Fatty a withering glance and continued. "We try to do our best not only to protect ourselves, but also our distinguished clients, such as yourself. I'm sure you will appreciate that."

Daguerre made a grudging sound.

"Good. Then everything is set. You have already made your full payment to Señor Blanco, so there is no more to do than explain your part in all this."

"I don't understand, Bill," Alex whined. "Why are we even involved in this aspect of it. Bart Sommers told us these people would bring our maid into the country for us. Why do we have to do *anything*?"

Hector Martinez smiled a perfect set of teeth. He took Alex's hand and patted it warmly. "Ah, Señora St. Clair, it is good to see a woman of such intelligence *and* beauty. It is true that we can take care of all the arrangements if you wish, but your husband insisted that delivery be made this week. We are only trying to comply with your wishes."

Daguerre nodded. "He's right, Sally. I can't bear for you to have to wash one more damn quiche dish."

"We have a dishwasher, Bill."

"Well, you still have to rinse them, don't you? And I didn't marry you so you could get rough flaking hands. Not when there are people who will do that sort of thing for you. You just work on your tennis backhand so we can crucify the Barnards next weekend."

Hector Martinez's smile widened, like a grandfather delighted with the antics of his grandchildren. But Daguerre knew the lines around Martinez's eyes weren't the kind that came from smiling.

"Your husband is quite right, Señora St. Clair. Life is too short to be bothered with the mundane. That is work for those born to it. However, if you insist on having your new employee so soon, you will have to help us a little. At no risk to you."

"What do you want us to do?"

"Simply drive a car home. That's all."

Alex looked at Daguerre, then back at Martinez. "You just want us to drive a car home?"

"That's all. Your employee—her name is Rosa—is hidden in the car. You will simply drive it home and leave the key under the driver's mat. Someone will pick up the car tonight."

"Where will Rosa be?"

"Inside the car. Don't worry, she will let herself out."

Daguerre and Alex stared at each other. "What do you think, honey?" Alex asked.

"Do not worry, Señora St. Clair," Martinez said with a dismissing laugh. "Even if the border guards catch you, they will simply send Rosa back home and we will bring her across later."

"But what will happen to us?" Alex insisted.

"Nothing. A warning at most. You can simply claim that you knew nothing about it. You had left your car parked on the street all day and someone must have used it unknown to you. Believe me, nothing will happen. Señor St. Clair, you are a lawyer. Am I not right about this?"

Daguerre nodded. "He's right, Sal. There isn't much risk at all. A little inconvenience is the worst that could happen to us."

"Okay. I just hope you're right."

Hector Martinez displayed his perfect teeth again. "Shall we get started?" He pressed a button on the wall and one of the garage doors began to creak open. The four of them walked outside to a tiny dirt parking lot where half a dozen cars were parked. Martinez marched straight to the black Mercedes sedan. "This is all yours, for the day. Registration is in the glove compartment. Everything is quite legal. The keys are in the ignition. Have a pleasant drive."

Alex stared at the car as she walked around it. "Where is she? In the trunk?"

Hector Martinez wagged his finger. "Tsk, tsk, *señora*. Suffice to say that you would be doing her a favor not to hit too many bumps."

Fatty chuckled at that until he started coughing.

Martinez hooked a thumb in Fatty's direction. "Asthma," he explained.

Daguerre and Alex climbed into the car. Alex couldn't help but look into the back seat as if she expected to find Rosa crouching there on the floor. Daguerre started the engine and noticed that the fuel tank was full. Very thoughtful.

"Do you know how to get to the border from here?" Martinez added.

Daguerre nodded. "I think so."

"Good. Well, Señor St. Clair, it was good doing business with you." He offered his outstretched hand to Daguerre, who reached his own through the open window. They shook hands and smiled at each other.

"Thanks for everything, Señor Martins," Daguerre said.

"Martinez," he corrected with an annoyed frown.

"Right. Thanks a lot. I'll be sure to tell my friends about you. You can count on that."

"Thank you. And remember, watch those bumps."

Daguerre waved and pulled out onto an alley which he followed to Second Street. He turned right, eventually swinging left onto Reforma.

They said nothing to each other as they approached the U.S. customs arch. Each was aware of another presence in the car, and rather than keep talking in character, they decided to say nothing.

They were waved through U.S. customs with a couple of brief questions from a bored official who was more interested in the fuel mileage of the Mercedes' diesel engine than in anything else.

They drove north on Interstate 5, keeping their conversation light and chatty, maintaining their roles as a wealthy pampered couple. Daguerre was even enjoying his part and he could see Alex was taking every opportunity to ham it up for their hidden guest.

"Really, Bill," Alex sighed wearily. "If the heat keeps up much longer, I'll simply *wither*."

"Whither thou goest, huggybear," Daguerre cooed.

Alex stuck her tongue out as if she would throw up and Daguerre had to keep himself from laughing. "Uh-oh," he said, pointing out the windshield as they approached San Clemente.

"What's up?"

"U.S. Immigration. They aren't going to be as easy as the customs folks."

The cars were moving slowly through the long lines, and more cars than usual were being pulled over to the side for inspection.

"Bill?" Alex said, a real tremble of concern in her voice.

"Nothing to worry about, dear," Daguerre soothed. "Every once in a while they get conscientious. No problem."

They inched slowly up in line, watching as some cars were waved through after a couple of questions, while others were being pulled over for thorough searches. When the Mercedes finally rolled up, a young customs official in aviator sunglasses stared into the car with a tight unsmiling face.

"Hi, Officer," Daguerre smiled. "What's going on? Big drug bust or something?"

The young man looked at Daguerre, ignoring the

question. Then he studied Alex, then peered into the back seat.

"Anything wrong?" Alex asked sweetly.

The customs official pointed to the side of the road. "Would you mind pulling over there and opening your trunk?"

22

The customs officer was only about twenty-three, but he took his job seriously. Though not so seriously that he neglected to steal as many appreciative glances at Alex's slender legs as he could.

"Do you have anything to declare, sir? Liquor, anything like that?"

Daguerre smiled charmingly. "Nothing, Officer."

The officer dashed a check mark on his clipboard. "Would you please open your trunk?"

"Certainly." Daguerre and Alex climbed out of the car, exchanged glances. They moved slowly toward the trunk, uncertain what they'd find there.

"What do we do?" she whispered nervously.

"We open the trunk."

"Christ."

Daguerre stuck the key into the lock, turned. The trunk lid popped open. Alex stood next to the trunk holding her breath as the customs officer lifted the lid higher. When the trunk door was open all the way, Alex was the first to stick her head in.

It was empty. Except for a worn catcher's mitt.

"My son's mitt," Daguerre quickly explained.

"A catcher, huh?"

"Yeah, well, he's a little too chunky for shortstop."

"Don't worry about it, sir," the young officer said. "I was a little chunky myself as a kid. Probably just baby fat." He patted his own stomach, which was flat and hard. He smiled shyly at Alex.

"Baby fat," Alex repeated numbly and climbed back into the car.

The customs officer gave her another once-over, licked his lips and waved them through.

They drove the freeway for another twenty minutes before anything was said. Alex turned to face Daguerre breathing freely for the first time. "Now what do we do? Just keep driving?"

"Nope."

"Well, then what?"

He swung into the right lane and took the next freeway exit. "I think it's time we got a look at our new maid."

23

It took about an hour of driving down deserted road after deserted road before Daguerre found an appropriately remote location. He pulled off the dirt road and drove across the sandy flats.

"This car does rather well in the sand," he said.

"I hope you know where you're going," Alex said, wiping sweat from her forehead. "The last sign we passed was for the town of Lizard Gap. What the hell kind of name is that for a town? And the sign. Did you notice there were a lot of holes in that sign?"

"Bullet holes."

"What?"

"The locals like to ride around in their pickup trucks and shoot the highway signs."

"What fun."

They drove deeper into the desert, the vegetation becoming sparser and the heat more intense. When Daguerre could no longer see any cars or buildings, he braked the Mercedes and shut off the engine. "Everybody out."

Alex quickly slid out her side of the car and stood a few feet away, watching. The icy expression on Daguerre's face gave her a nervous feeling that she wasn't going to like what was coming next.

Daguerre walked around to the side of the car and kicked it a few times. The metal dented with each kick. "You can come out now, Rosa." He leaned his arms against the hot black roof and peered into the back seat. Alex took a few tentative steps forward and also stared into the car.

They didn't have to wait long.

At the far end of the back seat, something poked up in the vinyl like a tent pole. Then it broke through with a popping sound. It was the short blade of a Swiss army knife, and it was now slicing the entire seat lengthwise.

A bare slender arm reached through, followed by a shoulder. Then a woman's head.

Alex gasped. "I feel like I'm watching this car give birth."

The woman squeezed her shoulders through the slit, then her torso, finally unfolding her legs. Daguerre swung the back door open and offered her a hand.

"Gracias," she said, smiling gratefully at him.

"De nada."

"Usted es muy amable."

"What'd she say?" Alex asked.

"She said that I was very kind."

"Boy, you don't waste any time do you, lover?"

Rosa smiled and curtsied at Alex. "I clean good for *señora*."

"Splendid," Alex said.

"Oh, you speak English, Rosa," Daguerre said with a friendly smile.

Rosa looked embarrassed and shuffled her feet, *"Sí, un poquito.* A little."

"Good, good. Much better than we had hoped for."

"Gracias." Rosa looked around at the endless stretch of desert around her. She frowned with a confused expression. "Why we stop here? Home?"

"No, no, dear child," Daguerre chuckled. "We were just concerned about you, that's all. We didn't want you to suffocate back there."

"Rosa fine," she said, her smile broader than Daguerre's. She was more than twenty-four years old, but had a hard leanness to her body. Her hair was thick and black, and she wore a pair of faded blue jeans, a white Mexican peasant blouse and leather sandals. There was no jewelry. No makeup. "We go now?"

"Yes, Rosa." Daguerre started for the car, then stopped and smiled again. "You know, that's an unusual accent you have."

"My English not so good," she apologized.

"I don't mean your English, Rosa. I mean your Spanish. You have an accent."

Rosa's smile was bigger than ever as she bobbed her head up and down. *"Sí,* Señor St. Clair. I from Mitla."

"Well, that explains it."

Alex looked confused. "Explains what?"

Daguerre stood with his hand on the door handle and explained. "Mitla is a little village about twenty-five miles to the south of Oaxaca. Next to the famous ruins. They have a wonderful hacienda-type restaurant there called...what was it, Rosa?"

Rosa opened her mouth to speak.

"Ah, yes," Daguerre interrupted. "Restaurant La Sorpresa. Terrific Mexican food. Anyway, Mitla was originally intended as a tomb for kings, high priests and the very noble."

"Lovely."

"The ruins are quite impressive. The patterns were made by cutting stones about four inches in length and then fitting them together perfectly so they would hold in place without cement of any sort. It's still a mystery of craftsmanship to modern stonemasons, eh, Rosa?"

Rosa shrugged. "Too fast, *señor*. You speak English too fast."

"Sorry. I'll slow down. Anyway, Rosa here comes from a village with a great history. Apparently she speaks an accent because Spanish is not her native tongue. She's a Zapotec Indian, a tribe that dates back to centuries before Christ. They still speak their native language. Right, Rosa?"

Rosa nodded.

Daguerre slapped the roof of the car. He turned back to face Rosa, who was standing next to the open door leading to the back seat. "This is even better than I thought, Rosa. You see, I had a chance to study some of the Zapotec language while in college. Ancient languages always fascinated me. I guess I'm an Indian buff, eh, Sally?"

Alex nodded. "I can't drag him away from the TV when *Broken Arrow* is on."

Rosa was still smiling, but her face seemed considerably paler.

Daguerre rattled off a few sentences in a language that Alex didn't recognize. "How's that, Rosa?" he asked with a proud grin.

"G-good, *señor*. Very good."

"I hope I didn't offend you, but college students always learn the dirty phrases first."

Rosa laughed. "*Sí*. I understand."

Daguerre glanced at his watch. "Well, we'd better be heading back to the freeway."

Everybody started to climb into the car, Rosa into the back. Suddenly Daguerre reached around the open door and grabbed Rosa, squeezing her neck with one hand and twisting her left arm high up between her shoulder blades with the other. Rosa struggled, kicking and wriggling, but none of it did any good. His grip was solid.

Alex came around the front of the car. "Not satisfied with her work already, dear? You're one tough employer."

"Well, I have certain standards," he said, wrestling Rosa to the ground. "I prefer that my employees wash windows, take out the trash and not belong to any terrorist organizations. Especially one run by Naif Nasil."

"Bite your tongue," Alex said.

Daguerre sat atop Rosa's chest, pinning her arms to her sides. She continued to struggle, but there was even less strength in her now. Daguerre whipped his belt from his slacks, rolled her over and began tying her hands behind her back. She made a vicious grab at his crotch and he clubbed her arm away.

Alex winced. "Take it easy, Chris."

"Don't go gooey on me now, Alex," Daguerre replied coldly. "I'm going to need you."

"Don't worry. I just don't think we have to overdo it."

Daguerre said nothing. He tore off his tie and wrapped it around Rosa's legs, knotting the loose end to the belt around her wrists.

"Oowww," Rosa moaned.

"Chris."

"She's okay. Aren't you, Rosa?"

Rosa scowled. "Pig! We will see who will pay for this."

"Hmm, your English has picked up quite a bit. At least it's better than your Zapotec."

Alex leaned against the car. "That reminds me, just what was that Zapotec mumbo jumbo you were spouting a few minutes ago? Where'd you learn that stuff, Mr. Know-it-all?"

"I didn't. I mean, I know about the language, but I can't speak it. I just figured that neither could she. I had to make certain before I made my move."

"You're sneakier than I thought, Chris."

Daguerre smiled at her. They both leaned against the car and stared at Rosa.

"Now what?" asked Alex.

"You search her."

"Me?"

"Yes. And look *everywhere*."

"What am I looking for?"

"Weapons, messages. We've got to find out what she and Nasil are up to."

Rosa laughed. "You will never find out. Not until it is too late. Not until the dead are counted up. And you will be among them."

"So will you if we don't get what we want." Dagger's voice left no doubt that he meant it.

Alex stooped over and began gingerly patting Rosa's pockets. She dipped her fingers into the right one and removed the Swiss army knife Rosa had used to cut through the back seat. Alex tossed the knife to Daguerre and continued her search.

"Everywhere," Daguerre said.

Alex started at the feet, pressing her hands along Rosa's legs, trying to feel for anything unusual under the material. Rosa had stopped struggling and was staring off into the distance. When Alex reached the more personal parts of Rosa's body, she apologized.

"I do not care," Rosa spat. "You are an American woman, and American women are dogs to men. Nothing more than whores and slaves."

"You must've met my last boyfriend."

"Search everywhere," Daguerre repeated.

"I did," she snapped, but searched Rosa again, feeling even more embarrassed now as she watched Rosa's smirking face.

Alex stood up, her face flushed. "There," she said angrily to Daguerre. "She's clean. You satisfied?"

"Are you?"

"I told you, she's clean. I don't know why you couldn't do it yourself."

"I'll show you why." Daguerre stooped down beside Rosa's head, reached into her hair and pulled out several hairpins. Then grabbed a handful of her hair and pulled. It came off. Rosa's real hair was short and wispy, though just as black as the wig.

"So, she's wearing a wig and I didn't notice. So what?"

Daguerre showed Alex the underside of the wig. Taped to the center with white adhesive tape was a shiny single-edged razor blade.

"Jesus," Alex whispered.

"That's right. She wasn't planning to shave her legs with it. Given the first opportunity, she would have used it to slit your throat. Or worse, mine. I just want you to see what we're dealing with here. Not your petty shoplifter.

"This woman was chosen to come up here because she's a killer. And the only reason they want killers is to kill. Whatever their plan is, it involves death. For how many, and whom, and when—that's what we have to find out. And that's what she's going to tell us."

Rosa's laughter was hard and metallic. "I will tell you nothing."

"We'll see," Daguerre smiled. "We'll see."

24

She was staked out spread-eagled on the baked ground, her arms and legs stretched as far apart as they would go. Her black hair was wet and matted against her forehead. Sweat soaked her blouse and pants with dark stains. Her eyes were closed against the bright sun, and she kept licking her dried lips, though there was no more saliva to moisten them.

Alex sat in the car and waited, automatically licking her lips whenever Rosa did. Daguerre had gone off twenty minutes ago, leaving her with the warning not to believe anything Rosa said.

"What are you," Alex had complained testily, "the exorcist or something?"

"In this case, yes."

But Rosa hadn't said anything since he'd left. She merely lay there silently enduring, at first struggling against the bindings, but finally just lying there. Alex couldn't help but admire her courage, wondering if she would have the same guts in a similar situation. Then she remembered the small house in Mazatlán, the three men about to rape and kill her. She'd held up pretty well, despite the numbing fear.

And now, looking at Rosa, about the same age as she, Alex felt somehow akin to her. She wondered for the first time whether Daguerre was doing the right thing.

She hopped out of the car and walked toward Rosa. "Why don't you just tell him what he wants to know, Rosa?"

"Stop calling me Rosa," she sneered. "My name is Sasha."

Alex stooped down and pleaded. "Tell, him, Sasha. You don't want innocent people to die."

Sasha blinked from the sun and Alex moved to the left to provide shade for Sasha's eyes. "You are very kind, Alex," Sasha said, her voice soft and warm. "I do not blame you for what you do. I know you only serve your male master."

"Damn it!" Alex bristled. "I don't have a master. Male or otherwise. I've been on my own for years, and I do what I do because I choose it. Because it's right. I don't want to see anyone die."

Sasha smiled kindly. "You have a good heart, Alex. You are not like the others. I will tell you a secret." She lowered her voice. "No one will die here."

"I don't understand."

"There is no plan, as your friend thinks. Naif Nasil is not even in this part of the world. He is back home fighting Israelis for our homeland. I let your master think what he wants. He would not believe me anyway."

"He's not my master!" Alex took a deep breath. "Never mind that. If there is no plot, then why are you and the others being smuggled into the United States?"

Sasha shrugged. "To hide for a while. Our faces are known by many. But no one would think of looking for us in the households of your wealthy. Even revolutionaries need to rest, to love, to feel human again. We are. no different than you, Alex."

Alex nodded sympathetically. It made sense.

"I hope you don't believe any of that crap," Daguerre said, stepping around the car. In his right hand was a handkerchief gathered at the corners and hanging upside down like an inverted parachute. There was something in it. Something moving.

"What have you got there, Chris?"

"One of nature's many helpful friends. Friends to some, anyway."

"Chris, what if she's telling the truth? All you have to do is tell the proper authorities and let them round the others up."

"If she were telling the truth that's exactly what I'd do. But she's not, Alex. There's something sinister going on. Something deadly. And if we try to round them all up, one's bound to slip through and set their plan, whatever it is, into motion. If it isn't already in motion. We can't take that chance. We have to *know*."

"But can't you see, what we're doing right now makes us as bad as them."

Daguerre stood in front of Alex and said quietly, "When's the last time you threw a bomb in a crowded restaurant, or machine-gunned a schoolbus full of kids, or shot some old judge's kneecaps off? Or cut somebody's tongue out?"

"That's a lie!" Sasha screamed.

"I've *seen* the victims," Daguerre said, his voice hollow and distant. "And I intend to make sure there aren't any more." He nodded at Alex. "Go wait by the car."

"But we're just reporters, Chris. We don't have the authority to do anything like this."

"I'm taking the authority."

"He's no reporter," Sasha snorted. "He's a government agent. Why else would he risk his life like this?"

Alex stared thoughtfully at Daguerre. "Is she right, Chris. Are you some kind of government agent?"

Daguerre sighed. "Did you ever see a newsreel of some man running down the street who's just been shot or was on fire or something?"

"Sure, all the time."

"Didn't you ever wonder how that cameraman taking the footage could just stand there photographing all that suffering without *doing* something to help?"

Her voice was quiet. "Yes."

"All right. I'm a reporter. And I know something is going to happen that will probably mean the deaths of many innocent victims. I could turn this all over to the 'proper authorities' and go home and write my little story, knowing the whole time that those authorities will probably be too late to stop the killing. Or I could do something *now* because it's the right thing to do. If that makes me a government agent, then I hope we're all government agents."

Alex hesitated, started to say something, then marched over to the car and waited.

Daguerre knelt beside Sasha and peeled open his handkerchief.

Sasha gasped and pulled away.

"My God, Chris," Alex cried.

Daguerre picked up the hairy orange-and-black tarantula by its back and held it a foot away from Sasha's face.

"Interesting creature," he said. "A member of the spider family Theraphosidae. I don't know where I come up with all this information. I guess journalists pick up a lot of trivia. Though I think my old biology teacher, Mr. Montand, would be proud of me."

Sasha tugged wildly against her bindings.

"I had a devil of a time finding one. They like to bury themselves underground, you know." He lowered the spider a few inches closer to Sasha's face. Its legs were thrashing in the air as if it were swimming. "Actually, these things are named after a town in Italy called Taranto. Their bite causes a disease known as tarantism, which makes the victim weep uncontrollably and then skip about in frantic circles. In fact—you'll find this amusing—that's where they get the name for that dance, the tarantella. Amazing, isn't it?"

Sasha groaned.

"What's particularly interesting is how many people have an absolute horror of spiders, especially this kind. What's that called again, something phobia? There's no telling who has it, anyone from construction workers to combat-hardened soldiers. I knew this one soldier who wouldn't get into his foxhole in the middle of the shelling because he'd seen a spider inside. He finally dropped a grenade into the foxhole before he'd get in. Arachnophobia! That's what it's called. Fear of spiders. Some psychologists believe we all have it to some extent or another."

Daguerre lowered the tarantula again. It dangled six inches above Sasha's mouth. "No, please," she whispered.

"This particular fellow is a *Eurypelma californicum*,

I believe. Of course, he's only a couple inches long with a leg spread of about five inches, but they have been known to get much bigger. Some even eat small birds.'' He lowered it again.

Sasha jerked back and tears mixed with sweat flooded her eyes. Some of the mucus drained back into her throat and she coughed. *"No!* Don't let it touch me!"

"Chris," Alex yelled. "Stop it."

Daguerre lowered the spider again. One of its wriggling hairy legs brushed Sasha's lips.

"Noooo! Please, I'll tell you. I swear. Please! Pull it away."

Daguerre lifted it an inch. "I'm listening."

She was panting like a distance runner. It took her a few seconds to catch her breath. "Naif is in Los Angeles somewhere. He is coordinating the operation. That's all I know."

Daguerre grabbed her jaw and squeezed, forcing her mouth open. Then he lowered the squirming spider halfway into her open mouth. "You tell me everything now or I'll drop it in and slam your mouth closed. I'll make you swallow the damn thing alive."

Sasha recoiled with a whimper, but nodded.

He pulled away.

She tried to wipe where the spider had brushed her lips on her shoulder but she couldn't reach. She took a deep breath and tried to compose herself. Her eyes never left the fat tarantula in Daguerre's hand. "I am not part of his operation, so I know little about it. He is a very brilliant man, but secretive. Everyone knows only what they must do. No more. It is safer for the operation that way."

"If you're not part of his operation, what are you doing here?"

"I am coordinating the next one. Everything depends upon the success of Naif's operation. It will be the first full-scale sanctioned terrorist activity in this country. When it succeeds, it will set off a chain reaction of other such terrorist attacks here. Once I learn of his success, I am to start my operation. When mine succeeds, the next leader starts his. And so on until we've forced your country to abandon the Zionists."

"What happens if Nasil fails?"

"If he fails we all withdraw and await further instructions. But he will not fail. He cannot. It is too close now."

"How close?"

Sasha hesitated.

"How close?" Daguerre lowered the thrashing spider.

"It is already happening. By tomorrow it will be over. That is all I know. I was not given the details."

Daguerre stood up and hurled the tarantula about twenty yards into the desert. It plopped onto a sand dune and scrambled away.

"That's all she knows," he said to Alex.

Alex walked toward him. "You were right, Chris."

"Yes, unfortunately. This is one time I would have preferred that you were right."

She leaned into his body and hugged him to her. "I'm sorry for sounding off back there. I guess I'm pretty damn gullible for a reporter."

"That's okay. You only asked the same questions I've asked myself. The questions you have to ask.

Maybe asking them is what makes the difference between us and them. Besides, you may be gullible, but you're tough.''

"I don't know, that was one ugly spider."

"Maybe," Daguerre grinned. "But quite harmless."

"Harmless? What about all that tarantella stuff and the skipping in circles?"

"Folklore. No truth whatsoever. Oh, these things can deliver a nasty little bite, but nothing serious. They make good pets, actually."

Alex stared at him a moment and frowned. "Sometimes I don't think I know you at all."

He smiled his most charming smile and kissed her forehead. "Now, let's get going. We've got some work to do."

"What are we going to do with her?"

"Give her to those 'proper authorities' you were talking about. You'll take her in while I look for Nasil." He tossed her the Swiss army knife. "Cut her loose and tie her hands behind her back. And be careful, she's a pro."

"What are you going to do?"

Daguerre pointed at the front left tire, which was about half flat. "Looks like we've developed a slow leak. I must have run over something on one of those dirt roads. Shouldn't take too long to fix."

He took off his jacket and draped it over the front seat of the car. Alex had already cut free Sasha's legs and was now unknotting the bindings around her wrists. Sasha sobbed slightly, spitting the sensation of the spider from her lips.

Daguerre leaned into the trunk and hoisted the spare tire out. He heard Alex shout.

"Chris!"

When he stepped around the car he saw what had happened. Somehow Sasha had managed to push Alex down and was now diving into the back seat of the Mercedes. Daguerre threw the tire aside and ran after her. He could see her arm lost in the slit opening of the back seat as he reached in to grab her ankles. But as he did, she twisted onto her back, her arm now out of the slit and gripping a Makarov pistol. She pointed it at Daguerre's mouth.

He dived to the ground just as the explosion sounded. A sharp sting bit the left side of his neck as if from a giant wasp. He was rolling now, trying to work his way around the back of the car and out of the line of fire. There were two more explosions and he could hear the bullets thumping into the ground near his head. Sand scraped his face as he rolled away.

Another scream ripped through the dry desert air, though this one was not from Alex. It was a high wail of surprise and horror that seemed to last for a full minute. Daguerre stopped rolling and sprang to his feet. He saw the blood and knew what had happened.

While Sasha had been concentrating on shooting Daguerre, Alex had shoved the car door into Sasha's body. When Sasha tried to turn the gun on Alex, Alex had thrust her Swiss army knife into Sasha's chest just below the sternum.

The knife was still sticking there as Alex kept slamming Sasha's hand with the gun against the roof of the Mercedes. Blood was bubbling up out of Sasha's mouth and dripping down her chin. Her eyes rolled and she sagged slowly to the ground.

Alex stood over her, holding the Makarov, breathing heavily, with tears running down both sides of her face. She stared wild-eyed at Sasha as if she thought it was some kind of trick, that any moment the body would leap up and attack her.

Daguerre examined Sasha's body.

"Is she dead?" Alex asked.

"Yes."

"Oh, God!" she cried, throwing down the gun and dropping to her knees, her chest racking with dry heaves.

Daguerre knelt beside her, holding her close, letting her cry. There was something hard and heavy in his stomach, as he rocked her back and forth on the hot sand. He was thinking about the sobbing relatives of a lot of victims. He was thinking about himself last year when Cara was gunned down. He was thinking about the relatives of the unknown victims to come if he couldn't stop Naif Nasil before tomorrow.

He remembered the first time he'd arrived in Vietnam as a reporter. The first thing he saw as he disembarked from the plane was a group of American GIs loading body bags onto another plane. One of the bags tore open and a severed leg dropped out. A nearby GI picked it up by the foot and stuffed it back into the bag without missing a beat of his gum-chewing. Daguerre's mouth had gone dry and another GI veteran standing next to him had laughed and said, "Welcome to the war, sonny."

Daguerre held Alex tighter and patted her hair. "Welcome to the war," he whispered.

25

Daguerre clamped the telephone receiver between his jaw and shoulder and listened to it ring. It pressed uncomfortably against the bandage on his neck where Sasha's bullet had nicked him, but he liked the discomfort. It kept his mind focused. While he waited, he finished loading William St. Clair's Smith & Wesson 9mm Model 39. Unfortunately, it was the only gun in the house.

"Yes?" The voice on the other end seemed weak and far away.

"Hello, Mr. Sommers? Mr. Bart Sommers?"

"Who is this?"

"Christian Daguerre, Mr. Sommers."

"Who?"

"Bill St. Clair."

"I don't know you."

"No, sir, I'm an acquaintance of Bill St. Clair."

"Yes, yes, St. Clair," the voice growled absently. "I know him. An attorney."

"That's right, Mr. Sommers. I was wondering if I might have a word with you?"

"About what?"

"Well, I'd rather discuss that in person."

"Hmm? What? I didn't hear you."

"I said I'd rather discuss that in person."

There was a pause. "I'm too busy right now. Can't see anyone. Call my office."

"I did, Mr. Sommers. They said you've taken a sudden leave of absence. An illness in the family."

"That's none of your goddamn business!" he shouted, and hung up.

Daguerre replaced the receiver and leaned back into the antique oak chair in St. Clair's study. The desk was also antique, a rolltop with every slot neatly filled and every paper neatly stacked. Daguerre resented such compulsive neatness and considered rearranging some of the papers. Instead he picked up the gun and box of 9mm cartridges and walked into the living room.

It was a magnificent house, complete with seven bedrooms and a maid's suite. The paintings were all quite expensive, though not very good. The furnishings were equally expensive, though they clashed with the design of the house. It was a home of people with much money, no taste and a desire to impress.

Daguerre flopped down on the overstuffed art deco sofa in front of the fireplace and considered his next move. There wasn't much time. Whatever was going to happen was going to take place within the next twenty-four hours. If not sooner.

At least Alex was out of the way. He'd checked her into the Beverly-Wilshire to wait, with a promise he'd give her the full story when it was all over. It had taken a little time to convince her that it would be best to bury Sasha in the desert for the time being. That any contact with the authorities would mean hours of questioning and requestioning. Hours that couldn't be spared.

It was all up to Dagger now. All he had wanted was a vacation in Mexico and instead he was sitting in a Beverly Hills mansion planning an attack against the most ruthless terrorists in the world. Perhaps his involvement was inevitable. Daguerre wasn't sorry. In a way he was grateful to Hannibal Kydd for giving him the chance to meet Cara's killer. He looked forward to confronting Naif Nasil. For one of them it would be his last confrontation.

Bart Sommers. He was the one who'd recommended the Maya Agencia de Viajes and their smuggling operation to the St. Clairs, and who knew how many others. He had written their letter of introduction, the one Daguerre had used in Cancun. Daguerre had hoped a personal interview with him might develop some lead. But Sommers had balked. Yet Sommers was a motion picture executive, used to high pressure. What had made him so nervous? So frightened?

Daguerre would have to find out.

He examined his pistol. It was a sad weapon, reliable only with full-metal-jacketed ammunition. Trigger pull was atrocious and accuracy was at best mediocre. But somehow police departments around the country had become enamored of them and ordered them by the gross, despite the fact that they often required extensive reworking before they could be issued to officers. It wasn't totally Smith & Wesson's fault, though. The pistol did quite well with the original 9mm military ammunition. But when modern high-performance 9mm loads were adapted, the gun lost its reliability.

Daguerre slipped the gun into his pants at the hollow of his back and shoved the box of shells into his jacket pocket. He sighed. There was no time to look for a better weapon. This one would have to do.

He walked back to the study and reread Bart Sommers's address from St. Clair's address book. When he'd memorized it, he tossed the book across St. Clair's desk, knocking stacks of paper into other stacks of paper. Some spilled onto the floor.

"Oops," he smiled.

26

Bart Sommers's house was even bigger than St. Clair's. It was walled in with giant leafy shrubs at least twenty feet tall. There was a long cobblestone driveway that sliced through a lush tropical garden, leading to the front door of the three-story Tudor-style house.

Daguerre parked the Mercedes and began ringing the doorbell. He could hear the bell sounding inside, but no one came to the door. He tried knocking for a while, but when that, too, brought no response, he slipped his American Express card between the door-jamb and door and worked it upward until the door sprang open.

He found Bart Sommers sitting alone in the living room, a half-empty bottle of Courvoisier on the glass-and-chrome table in front of him.

"Mr. Sommers?" Daguerre said.

"What the devil—" Sommers jumped up from the chair and teetered unsteadily. "How the hell'd you get in here?"

"The front door was wide open, sir. I thought something might be wrong."

Bart Sommers was a thick square man in his fifties, with small eyes sunk deep into gray folds of flesh. His nose was also thick, but it wasn't that of a drinker. Why then, Daguerre wondered, was he drunk this early in the afternoon.

"Who are you?" Sommers demanded.

"Christian Daguerre. We spoke earlier on the telephone."

"The telephone?"

"Yes. I'm the friend of Bill St. Clair."

"The attorney."

"Yes."

Bart Sommers scratched his curly gray hair. "Get out of here before I call the police."

"I don't think so, Mr. Sommers."

"You don't, huh?" He marched across the room to the phone and began pushing buttons. "Hello, police?"

Daguerre crossed his arms and waited as he'd done with the St. Clairs.

Sommers's face collapsed and he hung up the phone. "What do you want? Are you with *them*?"

"The kidnappers, you mean?"

Sommers nodded.

"No, I'm not."

"Then how did you know—"

"That your wife's been kidnapped?"

"Yes."

Daguerre took a few more steps and sat down on the chair across from Sommers. "I didn't, Mr. Sommers. I guessed. It wasn't too hard. You're a tough man in a tough business. It would take a hell of a lot to get you in this condition. Something personal. I noticed you're wearing a wedding ring but I don't see your wife around. Of course, she could be out shopping or something like that, but taking into consideration what I know about the people we're dealing with, I figure it's kidnapping.''

Sommers swigged another shot of cognac and scratched his unshaven face. His eyes were puffy and red. ''They've got Karen, too. My daughter. She's seventeen.''

''When's the payoff?''

''Are you FBI?''

Daguerre nodded.

''They made me swear not to call you guys in. Said they'd start sending me pieces of them. Hell, what could I do?''

''When's the payoff?'' Daguerre repeated.

He poured himself another glass of cognac, spilling some. ''I already made it.''

Daguerre angrily swept the glass and bottle off the table. ''When and where?''

''Hey, you can't—''

''When and where, Mr. Sommers?''

Sommers sighed. ''A few hours ago. I followed their instructions exactly. They said to have my gardener drive to a certain pay phone on Wilshire and they'd call him there with the rest of their instructions.''

''Your gardener?''

''Yeah, José.''

''Mexican?''

Sommers's facial muscles tightened slightly. ''Yeah, so what? You got something against Mexicans?''

''Only if they come from the Maya Agencia de Viajes.''

''How'd you—''

''And when they aren't really Mexicans, but PLO terrorists who are setting you up and probably a half a dozen others just like you for this kidnapping.''

"Wh-what do you mean?''

"You don't think you're the only one, do you? There's probably a whole group of wealthy families who have used the Maya Agencia's services. I'd bet if we called around to all the Beverly Hills banks we'll find there have been some substantial withdrawals over the past two days.''

"My God. You mean José is one of them?''

"He's probably the one who kidnapped your wife and daughter in the fist place and delivered them, and now the money, to his boss, Naif Nasil. When was the last time you spoke to your wife and daughter?''

"Right before I gave José the money. There was a phone call. They let them talk for a few seconds. They were both crying.''

Daguerre sighed. "Then there's a chance they're still alive. How much did you pay?''

Sommers hesitated, then spoke in a low choked voice. "Half a million. I had to borrow from friends. Call in a lot of favors. I even took some from the studio. If they ever find out—''

Daguerre saw Sommers's face go pale and his eyes bulge. His mouth dropped open as if to scream but nothing came out. Daguerre swung around, his hand already reaching for the Smith & Wesson in his belt. He dropped to the floor in time to see the skinny olive-skinned man in gardener's overalls pointing his gun. But it wasn't a Makarov pistol this time. It was a Heckler & Koch MP5 submachine gun, capable of firing 100 9mm parabellum cartridges per minute on full automatic.

"José," Sommers finally said. Then his face reddened with anger and he leaped up, kicking the spilled cognac bottle out of his way. "Where the hell's Julie and Karen, you son of a—"

Then José squeezed the trigger and the room echoed with clattering explosions.

27

Bart Sommers caught the first burst in the legs. The force of the bullets chewed away cloth, flesh and bone, sending him sprawling face forward into the glass-and-chrome table. The glass top shattered on impact, and Daguerre could see jagged shards of glass imbeded in Sommers's face and neck. Blood from his mangled legs soaked into the plush white carpet.

José fired another burst into the chair Daguerre was crouching behind. Tufts of stuffing and wood snowed over Daguerre's head and shoulders.

He waited patiently for the burst to end, then popped up and squeezed off a single round from the S & W. The bullet went wide by six inches, but it surprised José enough to force him to take cover around the dining-room corner.

Daguerre cursed his gun. There wouldn't be many clean shots, and he'd already blown one. Eventually José was going to figure out that even in an isolated house like this someone might hear and report the shots. Then he would step around that corner and blast Daguerre's chair to dust. And Daguerre with it.

Sommers moaned and started to push himself off the table. The cuts weren't too serious, but they were bleeding a lot. Some of the blood ran into his eyes and he tried to wipe it away, smearing his face as if with war paint. "My legs," he gasped.

"Stay down!" Daguerre said.

Then the room exploded again. A dozen rounds tore through the chair and the chrome goosenecked lamp next to it. Dust hung in the air like a fog.

"Jesus," Sommers said, hugging the floor. "I think I'm hit again. My goddamn hip. I can't feel nothing."

Daguerre didn't answer.

"Hey, man, you okay?"

Daguerre hunched behind the chair and groaned. "I'm...hit...too."

"Oh, no. How bad?"

"Bad," Daguerre said weakly. "I...I can't... move."

"Jesus. Toss me the gun."

"I...can't...."

Daguerre counted slowly.

One.

Two.

Three.

At three, he jumped up with gun outstretched and began firing at the corner of the dining room.

The first bullet caught José just as he stepped out, thinking that both his adversaries were immobile and anxious to finish them off. Daguerre's bullets pummeled José's shoulder twice, smashing his collarbone and spinning him around into the wall.

Daguerre leaped over what was left of the shredded chair and tackled José to the floor.

José struggled, groping for his submachine gun, which had tumbled away when he'd fallen. But Daguerre drove his elbow down into José's shattered shoulder. The terrorist screamed.

"Where are they?"

Bart Sommers crawled across the carpet, dragging his mashed useless legs behind him. "I'll make him talk," he growled. He grabbed the Heckler & Koch submachine gun, digging the butt into the carpet to pull himself closer. When he was less than a foot away he stuck the barrel in José's face, pressing it against the man's forehead. "Talk José, or whatever the hell your name is. Talk or I swear I'll spray your face all over this floor."

Daguerre climbed off José's chest. "Let's take a look at you first, Mr. Sommers." He bent over and examined the bleeding wounds.

"I'll live," Sommers said, wincing under Daguerre's probing fingers.

Daguerre smiled. "Damn right you will. But we'd better get an ambulance here right away. Those legs are going to need surgery."

"First we make him *talk*. If he knows an ambulance is on the way he'll try to hold out. He knows the cops will never be able to make him talk."

"Well, the FBI—"

"And don't give me none of that FBI jazz, pal. From what I've just seen, it's obvious you aren't with any FBI. And as for my legs, a few minutes aren't gonna matter much anyway, are they?"

Daguerre got up and raced down the hall. When he came back he had two leather belts for tourniquets. "This will stop the bleeding for a while." Daguerre went to work tightening the belts around Sommers's legs. None of the wounds were fatal, but he'd be surprised if Sommers would ever walk again. Sommers seemed to know that already. In the meantime, there wasn't any time to lose in making José talk.

Daguerre snatched the submachine gun from Sommers and stood straddling the gardener. José sneered up at him. He was a couple of years younger than Daguerre, with small nervous eyes. Daguerre pointed the gun at José's face. "Where did you take the money?"

José spat at the gun. His saliva was mixed with a little blood. Some of the pink foam hung on his lips. "I will tell you nothing."

Daguerre kicked José's wounded shoulder. The man screamed with bared teeth, but said nothing.

"I don't have time for inventive torture. So it's going to be pure brute force. But even with brute force you'll talk." He kicked the shoulder again, harder.

José's scream was piercing, like some African bird, but still he wouldn't talk.

"Let me try," Sommers said. "I'll make him talk."

"You'll kill him, and I don't want him dead."

"But he knows you won't kill him. Why should he talk?"

"Some things are worse than death. Just leave it to me if you want your family back."

Sommers nodded resignedly. "I don't understand why he came back. He had the money."

"Simple," Daguerre said. "Since you had no idea he was involved, it was safe for him to come back here and wait."

"Wait for what?"

"Wait until the money was checked out. Make sure it wasn't marked or anything. It takes awhile to run it through all the tests. Chemicals, ultraviolet light, and such. Once they were sure it was all okay, he'd get a signal. Maybe the phone would ring twice and then stop."

"Signal?"

"To kill you. Get rid of the loose ends. Imagine, not only do they make a fortune to help finance their activities, but more important, they get all this publicity on how they slaughtered a group of rich capitalists. Right, José?"

"You will *all* die soon enough," José snarled.

"Perhaps," Daguerre said, "but not soon enough to do you any good." Daguerre pointed the gun at the terrorist's crotch. "Say goodbye to your manhood, José."

He gasped and closed his eyes.

Daguerre adjusted the angle slightly and fired. Bullets pounded into the floor between José's legs, kicking up puffs of white carpeting.

"It's a good thing you didn't move, boy," Sommers grinned.

"Where are they?" Daguerre asked.

José shook his head, but there was no more defiance in his manner. Some things *were* worse than death. At least in death one could be a martyr for the cause. But there was no honor in castration. Only shame. Ridicule.

"Have it your way," Daguerre shrugged and fired again. Several bullets singed the inside of José's thighs. They bled slightly.

He moaned. Sweat had boiled out across his forehead and neck. "Kill me!" he demanded. "Kill me, you filthy pig. Kill me. I am not afraid to die."

"I'm not going to kill you," Daguerre said. "I'm just going to, uh, change you a little. Altered states, you might call it." He fired again. The bullets cut higher on the inner thigh, closer to the crotch.

"Sentry!" José screamed.

"What's that?"

"A boat. In Newport Beach. That's where I took the women and the money."

"Is Naif there?"

"No."

"Where is he?"

"I don't know. The man on the boat is to deliver the money to Naif when it has all come in. Only he knows where Naif is. Now kill me. I demand it!"

"What will be done with the hostages?"

José said nothing.

He didn't have to.

Daguerre handed the gun and telephone to Sommers. "Call the ambulance first for yourself. Then call the police for him."

"Are you kidding me?"

"Just tell them he's a burglar. The less they know about the kidnapping, the better my chances of saving your family."

"You're asking for a lot of trust."

"I've earned it."

"Yeah," Sommers nodded. "What about you?"

"I'm going down to Newport Beach."

Bart Sommers stared at Daguerre for a few seconds. Then he smiled and nodded. "Okay, sure. I'll call them."

Daguerre jogged out of the house, started up the Mercedes, and was halfway down the long winding driveway before he heard a faint burst of gunfire from the house. It wouldn't bring Sommers's legs back, but it would make living without them a little easier.

28

The man with the green visor and the Mickey Mouse T-shirt opened his door, squinted at the figure before him and shook his shaggy head in disbelief. "Oh, no. Not you. Not now."

Daguerre smiled. "Hello, Jimmy. Miss me?"

"Is a pope Catholic?" Jimmy swung his door open and waved Daguerre in. "My house is your house," he said grudgingly.

"Considering how much money you owe me from the last poker game we were in, that's probably true."

"Come on, Chris, you have my marker. And I send you a check every month."

"Every other month."

"Really? It seems like every month."

Daguerre looked around the sparsely furnished living room. There was one battered and torn chair and a cheap coffee table usually found in $7-a-night motels. The draperies were drawn and there were no lights on. "You just move in here?"

Jimmy nodded. "Yeah, about four years ago. I'm still unpacking. Drink?"

"No time, Jimmy. I'm in a hurry."

"Uh-oh. Sounds serious."

"It is."

"How serious?"

"Four or five hands' worth."

"Damn!" He rubbed his bloodshot eyes. "Okay, okay. Let me tell the guys." Jimmy shuffled to the doorway in his bare feet and called down the hall. "Deal me out a few hands, guys. I've got business."

A voice called back. "You've got business here, Jimmy."

"Yeah, monkey business," someone else said.

There was some laughter.

Jimmy turned around and walked to the stereo, flicking on a record. Mick Jagger began singing "Angie."

Jimmy stared at the record a few seconds and sighed.

"Angie leave you again?" Daguerre asked.

"Fourth time in a year. This one looks like the real thing, though. She got her own apartment in Long Beach this time; someplace where you have to pay first *and* last month's rent. She never went that far before."

"I called Ed Banks at the *Times*. He said you didn't come in today."

"Did he cover for me?"

"I don't know. But he said you've been doing this more and more. He figures they're bound to fire you by the end of the year."

Jimmy shrugged. "Man does not live by journalism alone. He needs poker."

"That's your business. I'm just looking out for my investment. You owe me."

The song was over and Mick began singing another one. Jimmy hopped up from the floor and started "Angie" over again. "Women," he mumbled.

Jimmy Linder was Daguerre's age, but he looked at

least ten years older. They'd met in Vietnam as rival reporters. Jimmy had been a 4-F reporter anxious to prove he wasn't afraid of combat. He was also the worst poker player in Southeast Asia, and therefore was invited to every military and civilian poker game in the country. He always accepted. And he always lost.

"So, what's up?"

Daguerre leaned forward in the chair. "I'm trying to track down a boat. It's in Newport Beach. I need the exact location."

"Jesus, you don't ask for much."

"It's important."

Jimmy sat on the edge of the coffee table and studied Daguerre's face. "Right. What kind of boat is it?"

"I don't know. Why?"

"Well, if it's a motorboat or a sailboat over twenty-six feet it has to be registered with the state. That would make things a lot easier."

"I'm not really sure, but considering what they're using it for, it would have to be one of those."

"Okay. What's the name of the boat? You do know that, I hope."

"The *Sentry*."

Jimmy rubbed his red eyes and squinted at Daguerre, "Okay. I'll see what I can do. I've got a friend at the Department of Motor Vehicles. Well, she's a friend of Angie's really. But I did fix her up a couple times with dates that didn't drool on her too much, so she owes me. She's come through for me before. Hang on." He got up and shut off the record player, then wandered into the kitchen. He was gone for fifteen minutes.

"Come on, Jimmy," someone shouted from down

the hall. "And bring your pink slip for your Mustang. My kid's graduation is coming up."

Jimmy came back with a torn piece of telephone book cover. "Here's the location. It's moored just off Balboa peninsula. Its registration number is CF-9215-GG. It's a twenty-eight-foot Bertram Flybridge Cruiser. Nice little boat, registered to Pedro Fuente." He handed the torn cover to Daguerre. "Anything else?"

Daguerre stood up and stuffed the cover into his pants pocket. "Yes. How do I get back on that damn freeway."

Jimmy laughed and gave him directions. "Got it?"

"Yes."

"Just remember to get on Pacific Coast Highway to get to Balboa. The rest is easy."

They shook hands. Jimmy led Daguerre to the door and clapped him on the back. "Maybe when you've taken care of whatever you're doing you might come back for a little social call. Like dinner or something. I'll call Angie. She'd love to see you again."

"Definitely. Call her now and set it up for tomorrow night. Make reservations somewhere nice. For four."

"Four?" He raised his eyebrows and grinned. "Someone special?"

Daguerre smiled. "See you tomorrow." He started out the door, then turned back. "By the way, this makes our debt clean."

"But—"

"Give my love to Angie," Daguerre said quickly and hurried to the car.

When he climbed into the black Mercedes he flipped open the glove-compartment door and pulled out the

Smith & Wesson. He reloaded the clip, slipped it back into his pants at the hollow of his back and pulled away from the curb. He hoped Angie would pick the restaurant instead of Jimmy. He hoped it would be Le St. Germain restaurant on Melrose.

He hoped he would still be alive to enjoy it.

29

It looked like a giant clothespin.

One side of the pin was the endless string of hot sandy beaches: Huntington Beach, Newport Beach, Corona del Mar, each with its share of volleyball nets, wet-suited surfers, and scantily clad girls. On the other side of the pin was skinny little Balboa peninsula, where the smallest of houses could rent for $800 a week during the prime summer months. Floating between these two strips of land was Balboa Island. And the Newport Bay.

Daguerre stood on one of the docks on Balboa peninsula and looked around. To his left, almost around the bend, a ferry was chugging four cars and a dozen people from the island to the peninsula. Another ferry was going in the opposite direction. To his right he could see the game arcade and snack shops filled with milling people eating corn dogs and cotton candy. An elderly couple in their late sixties rollerskated by.

Across the bay the U.S. Coast Guard station sat next to the Orange County Harbour Department. Docked in front of the buildings was a huge white Coast Guard cruiser, the *Point Divide*, with a skinny blond boy polishing the guns. Two smaller gray harbor-patrol boats were docked to the right of the cruiser, while to the left were three yellow lifeguard boats with "Rescue" stenciled in blue across the cabins.

Daguerre thought for a moment about going to them, explaining everything. But he knew what would happen. Delays. Questions. Phone calls trying to find someone to take responsibility for a decision. The hostages on the *Sentry* couldn't wait that long.

Even if he could enlist their help, at the first sign of a uniform or approaching boat, the hostages would likely be killed. It was difficult explaining to some officials that dealing with terrorists was not like dealing with drug runners. It took a special experience. And Daguerre, God help him, had that experience.

He looked at his watch. It was almost six o'clock and the sun was still bright. The air was cool from the sea breeze, but it was comfortable. Relaxing. The people around him were all smiling, enjoying themselves, the weather, each other. It was not a place for what had to be done now.

Daguerre studied the hundreds of boats and ships docked and moored along both sides of the bay. Millions of dollars' worth just floating calmly on gentle swells. Even though their boats were tied up, some people were sitting on deck sipping from glasses and staring at the other boats returning from sea.

And there were plenty of them of all sizes. Many of the sailboats had brightly decorated spinnakers. Daguerre recognized a famous movie star at the wheel of one cruiser as it sped by. Darting between these crafts were tiny windsurfers, skimming back and forth across the bay like water spiders. Each had a different colored sail and each person risked their already precarious balance by pulling their sail against the wind for more speed.

"Ever try it?" asked a man at Daguerre's side.

Daguerre nodded. "A couple times. In France."

"Sure, France. We sell them there." The man hooked a thumb over his shoulder. Daguerre looked back in that direction. "That's my store. Caldwell's Windsurfers. Factory outlet. I shipped three of them to Germany last summer. Frankfurt."

Daguerre said nothing. He was scanning the identification numbers painted on the bows of the ships.

"Wouldn't be too hard to ship one. Where you from?"

"Death Valley."

"Oh." The man pulled out a cigarette, lit it and wandered up to a young couple about twenty feet away. "Ever try it?" he asked them.

Daguerre found it quickly. The bow was turned away from him, but the name on the transom was clear: *Sentry I*. It was a Bertram Flybridge Cruiser with closed curtains around the entire cabin. There was no one on deck.

He felt his pulse quicken. A thin film of sweat coated his fingers. The gun wedged against his back seemed suddenly heavier, almost insistent. He had to get aboard.

But there was a problem.

The boat was not docked, it was moored. That meant the owner rented space in the water where he could tie up his ship. With limited dock space, this was becoming more and more popular, especially because it was significantly cheaper. But it was also harder to approach.

Daguerre stared grimly at the boat, as if he thought he might will himself aboard. If only there was more time. He could think of half a dozen plans to get himself on that ship. But each took equipment, disguises, falsified papers. There just wasn't enough time for such subtlety. But an obvious approach would insure the hostages' deaths.

He stared at the boat for fifteen minutes without moving. Finally, something like a smile played at his lips.

"Yes," he said quietly. "Yes, that should do it."

30

Paul Caldwell of Caldwell Windsurfers looked confused. "You don't want me to ship it over to Death Valley or wherever?"

"I'll take it with me," Daguerre explained.

"But where can you use it there? It's all desert."

"That's the challenge."

Caldwell shrugged. "You want some help loading it up? You can park in the alley here and—"

"No. I want to use it now."

Caldwell scratched his neck. "That's a first."

Daguerre handed him his American Express card.

"Looks a little chewed up around the edges."

"I used it to jimmy a locked home in Beverly Hills."

Caldwell nodded solemnly. "That explains it, then."

When Daguerre had signed the slip, he said, "I have a few more purchases to make. I'll be back in fifteen minutes. I'd appreciate it if you'd have the mast and sail together for me."

"Sure thing, mister."

Twenty minutes later, Daguerre pushed off from one of the private docks on Balboa peninsula. He was no longer wearing his light cotton suit or carrying William St. Clair's Smith & Wesson. Instead, he wore Adidas swimming trunks and a long-sleeved wet-suit jacket.

Tucked inside the left sleeve of the jacket was an eight-inch diver's knife with a blue rubber handle. All courtesy of American Express.

The sky was not as bright as it had been only half an hour ago, and Daguerre could see the sun reflected in the giant plate-glass windows of the million-dollar homes that lined both sides of the bay. Behind those silky windows, important people were sitting down to eat salt-free low-cholesterol meals, and servants were waiting to wash dishes and watch TV.

There were fewer people walking bayside now, but a couple of the curious stopped to watch Daguerre mount his windsurfer. From the edge of the water, Daguerre heard Caldwell accosting them with, "Ever try it?"

Windsurfing is a lot like walking, Daguerre thought, once you know how, you can't remember ever not knowing how. It is a cross between surfing and sailing, both of which Daguerre was adept at. He anchored his feet on either side of the mast for good balance and began pulling on the uphaul rope until the mast was out of the water. Then he grabbed the aluminium boom and tilted the sail into the wind. The windsurfer began picking up speed until it was skipping over the water toward the group of boats that were moored in the middle of the bay. The *Sentry* was among them.

Daguerre had debated about the gun, but there was no way he could take the chance of its bulk being spotted under the wet-suit jacket. If it was, he'd be dead—and so would the hostages. The knife would have to do.

The wind was not blowing as steadily as it had earlier, so his progress was not very rapid. He slowed down several times, once stopping dead in the water. But he continued tacking and jibbing toward his target.

Boat traffic was down to a weak trickle now, and there were only two or three other windsurfers left in the cold water. One man was obviously a beginner and was having trouble making it back to shore. Every ten feet he'd fall off the board with a loud splash and curse.

As Daguerre moved closer to the *Sentry*, he saw that the cabin curtains were still drawn, even around the windshield. There was no light inside. No movement anywhere.

He maneuvered the little windsurfer at a proper angle to both the wind and the *Sentry*, then tilted the mast and sail forward. The windsurfer began to pick up speed. He tilted it further, forcing it even faster toward the hull of the boat.

Daguerre could taste the salty wind as it puffed into his sail, propelling him forward at a greater and greater speed. He was bent backward at a forty-five-degree angle, clutching the boom to his chest. The *Sentry*'s hull loomed larger as he raced toward it. Faster and faster. Closer and closer.

And then the crash.

The windsurfer rammed the boat with a hollow thud. The impact was great enough to send Daguerre somersaulting over the side of the board. He let out a loud hoarse yell, hoping to attract the attention of whomever was inside the boat.

"Help!" he yelled as he clawed his way to the surface, gulping for air in his best imitation of a drowning man. Still, no one aboard stirred. If there was anyone aboard. One way or the other, Daguerre would find out.

"Help!" he called again, banging on the hull.

No response.

He dived down into the murky water and tied his up-haul rope to the anchor cable attached to the mooring buoy, at the same time lodging the mast between the cable and the buoy. When he came up again, he pounded the hull with his fist and shouted, "Someone on the *Sentry*. I'm injured and my sail's stuck. Can you help me?"

Silence.

"I'm unable to free my mast," he shouted again. "I'll have to come aboard."

He reached up, grasped the edge of the transom, and began pulling himself up.

Immediately the cabin door aboard the *Sentry* slammed open and shut again, and a large hand was prying his fingers from the transom.

"Get the hell away!" the accented voice barked. He was a young man with a thick black beard and a nose that had been broken often, but never set. It leaned to the left, making it seem as if he talked out of the side of his mouth. His eyes were also black, and they glared down angrily into Daguerre's.

"I'm hurt, pal," Daguerre said.

"Tough. Now get the hell away from here." He pried another of Daguerre's fingers loose.

"I can't. My mast is tangled up in your mooring cable. I've wrenched my shoulder and can't work it loose. Maybe if you give me a hand."

"I am giving you ten seconds." He reached down behind the transom. When he brought his hand up again it was curled around a short gaff with a long metal hook at the end.

Daguerre looked properly frightened. "Well, let me get my friend over there to help me." He turned and shouted to the beginning windsurfer who'd just taken another spill. *"Hey, Bill!"*

The beginner looked over in Daguerre's direction. Daguerre waved and nodded. The beginner waved back.

"He'll send help. I'll just wait here on my board till they come and get me. But I'm telling you now, buddy, I'm going to have to report you for not helping me out. It's some kind of maritime law, you know."

"Push off, mister, before I turn on the engine."

Daguerre could feel the still T-233 MerCruisers' propellers under his treading feet. If they were turned on they'd chew his legs off. He let go of the transom and slid the rest of the way into the water. "You'll hear from my lawyer," Daguerre shouted.

The bearded man went back inside the cabin, slamming the door behind him.

Well, it hadn't worked. They were being more careful than he'd expected. At least it confirmed that there was something on board to hide. There was only one option left now, and Daguerre didn't like it.

It had to be done quickly, with one fluid motion, because as soon as he touched the boat again the man with the beard and gaff would be back. *What the hell?* Daguerre thought and dived down.

He went down ten or fifteen feet, curled himself into a tight ball, then sprang upward, swimming toward the surface with hard kicks. When he broke through the surface he reached his hands up over his head, hooked them around the transom and hoisted himself over the edge and into the *Sentry* with a soft thud.

ne cabin door flew open and the man with the beard was running at him, the silver gaff swinging over his head like a club. It hissed through the air over Daguerre's head, but came close enough to ruffle his hair. There was no mistaking this man's intent to kill him.

Daguerre rolled across the deck into the ladder that led to the flybridge above the cabin. The gaff hissed again, clanging against the aluminium ladder. During the roll, Daguerre finally managed to work his knife free just in time to parry another swing from the gaff. He was on his feet now, sidestepping the thrusts, threatening with his own knife.

The man with the beard frowned with each missed swing, concentrating more intently. Daguerre looked around to see if anyone from shore was noticing what was going on. But most of the crowds were gone by now, and there were so many other moored boats surrounding them, blocking the view from the shore. The only person that was paying any attention was the beginner floating on his windsurfer. But he was unable to do anything about it.

"Arrgg," the bearded man yelled and thrust the gaff at Daguerre's chest. Daguerre slipped to the right and the thrust missed him, but when the man pulled the gaff back, the hook caught Daguerre from behind, piercing his wet suit and upper left arm. The bearded man smiled at his luck and tugged harder. Daguerre felt his flesh and muscle tearing. The pain numbed his right arm.

The man pulled harder and the metal hook was dripping with blood now. He couldn't unhook Daguerre's arm, so he decided to rip the entire length of the arm. He jerked it again.

Daguerre grunted and tried to grasp the gaff handle with his right hand, but the gaff jerked again and was out of reach. He felt the warm blood dripping down his arm and side inside the wet suit. Thick red rivulets flowed out the sleeve and webbed down his hand.

Clutching the knife in his right hand, he waited for the inevitable. When the next tug came he leaped forward with the force, wrapping his left hand around the gaff as he charged ahead. The man with the beard tripped backward off balance and Daguerre was on him, his diver's knife plunging through flannel shirt, skin, rib and muscle, slicing upward through the lung and finally into the heart.

Daguerre ignored the suction of the man's organs on his knife as he pulled it slowly out. He was trying not to disturb the hook through his upper arm. The hook was barbed, so he couldn't pull it out the way it had gone in. He'd have to pull the whole hook all the way through. Carefully he unscrewed the gaff handle from the hook, grinding his teeth against the burning pain. Fortunately it was a small gaff, so the hook was not too thick. When it was detached, he eased and coaxed the metal through the hole in his arm.

He dropped the bloody hook over the side. In the twilight distance he saw the beginning windsurfer sitting on the edge of his board and staring at him with disbelief.

Daguerre bent over the body. It wasn't Naif Nasil, that much he knew. Nasil was much older, a couple of years older than Daguerre. And of course there was that famous burn scar across the forehead like a comet, the result of a bomb he'd planted exploding too soon. But this is where José the gardener had delivered the money

and the hostages, so this was where Daguerre would
start.

He staggered over to the cabin door and pushed it
open. Inside on the floor, huddled in a small shivering
circle, were more than a dozen bound-and-gagged
women and children. Their feet were tied and then
lashed to the cabin's bolted chairs and tables. There was
the strong smell of urine, probably from the children
unable to control their bowels any longer.

And piled in the middle of their ragtag circle were
eight bulging duffel bags. One of the bags was open and
packets of twenty-dollar bills had spilled out.

Daguerre stepped into the cabin, stooping to untie the
closest woman. He saw her eyes widen as she pulled
away and shook her head fiercely. A surge of adrenaline
electrified his stomach. He turned his head in time to see
the wooden club cracking into his skull.

And behind the club, a scar across the forehead like a
blazing comet.

31

Daguerre felt the fish nibbling at his face. It was an annoying feeling, yet strangely comforting. As if they were nudging him. Encouraging him. Maybe it was worth taking a look.

He opened his eyes.

The fish was a foot. In a size eight ladies' tennis shoe. Nike. It belonged to the woman he'd stooped over to untie when he'd entered the cabin. She was kicking at him, her eyes red-rimmed and urgent, her yelling muffled by the gag around her mouth. Others were also grunting, and at first the sound of all that grunting made Daguerre want to laugh.

Then he remembered the scar.

Centaur!

His head throbbed as if it were continually swelling and deflating, each time swelling more and deflating less. He touched his fingers to his forehead. They came back drenched in sticky blood.

The foot kicked his chin.

"Mmmmph!" she said.

Daguerre crawled to her, removing her gag. She gasped for air. "Stop...him...gotta...stop...."

Daguerre's hands automatically curled around his nearby knife. He cut through her ropes.

"No time..." she said, pushing away at his hands as he tried to also free her feet. "No time. He has the boat rigged...bomb. They talked about it. Detonator on other ship."

"Other ship?"

"Hurry!" she pleaded.

Then Daguerre understood everything. This was *Sentry I*, there was probably a *Sentry II*. And if this ship was rigged to explode, with the detonator on the other ship, they had probably planned to transfer the money to the other ship, sail out of the bay and explode the *Sentry I* when they were a safe distance. The chaos would allow them a clear escape to Mexico, complete with about $6-million in cash. Daguerre looked around and saw the ultraviolet light on the table. They'd been in here checking to make sure the bills weren't marked before they left. The ultimate terrorist act: killing innocent victims while making a $6 million profit.

Daguerre jumped to his feet, handing the knife to the woman. "You do the rest. Just free the feet then get everybody overboard. At least they'll be able to tread water."

He ran through the cabin door. Nasil had jumped overboard and was swimming toward an identical boat docked across the bay. His strokes were smooth and powerful, and he was less than thirty yards from *Sentry II*.

Daguerre leaped overboard, immediately feeling the sting of salt water on his gashed arm and swollen head. He dived down to loosen the mast of the windsurfer from the mooring cable, but his wounded arm made it harder for him to hold his breath. He came up for air.

His head was dizzy and he could feel the thick lump bulging under his scalp.

He dived again. This time the mast swung free and he was able to climb on the board. The polyethylene was scratching beneath his feet, keeping him from slipping. He hoisted the mast and sail, tilted it into the wind, and was soon racing across the bay. To make it go faster required more strength, for he had to tilt the sail deeper into the wind, but he was uncertain how much pressure his torn and bleeding arm could take. Still he had no choice.

He tilted the mast further.

The windsurfer picked up more speed, bucking under his grip, trying to pull free. He leaned backward until his body hovered less than a foot above the water. Daguerre felt warm blood pumping from the wound, saw it drip onto his feet, onto the white board. He sped faster across the bay, closing the gap between Nasil and himself.

Then the wind began to die.

At first it was a slight slowing, then it was gone altogether. The windsurfer lay dead in the water. Daguerre stood on the useless board, clutching the limp sail, and watched his adversary escaping. Nasil was less than ten yards from his boat and Daguerre was more than thirty.

He couldn't stand here waiting for another breeze to come along. It might be too late.

Without hesitation, he let the sail flop onto the water and dove off the side of the board. The swimming was difficult. Each time he lifted his left arm the pain jolted along his nerves like an electrical shock. But he kept swimming, his arms adopting a rhythm of their own, something beyond his body. Something hypnotic. Soon each arm *had* to cut into the water, each *had* to pull him further. They had no choice. It was a Zen technique he'd learned in Asia, but he was not a master so it was only good for a few minutes. After that, the pain would be doubled.

He lifted his head from the water in time to see Nasil pulling himself over the transom and into the boat. Daguerre was less than fifteen yards away now. The Zen technique was starting to fail and the pain was now twice as great as it had been. He bit down hard on the inside of his cheek, using that pain to keep his attention away from his failing arms.

Almost there.

Nasil's wet sneakers padded across the boat's deck. His bronzed wiry body moved with the quick strength of a gymnast as he hopped up the ladder to the flybridge platform ten feet above the deck and fumbled with the boat's controls. The motors at the back of the boat whipped the water with a rumbling growl.

Next he grabbed the key he wore around his neck, stooped over, and began unlocking the cabinet next to the wheel. Instinctively Daguerre knew what was in that cabinet.

The detonator.

By the time Daguerre reached the boat, the propeller blades were furiously churning water behind the transom. Climbing aboard was much harder from the side of the ship where it rode higher out of the water, especially when he had only one good arm. But Daguerre did it. He pulled and kicked with his feet, walking his way up the hull until he rolled over the edge onto the deck.

His arm flamed with pain, but he tried to ignore it as he scrambled for the ladder.

He was three rungs up when he saw Nasil suddenly lean over the edge of the platform, aiming the flare gun at his face. The gun exploded just as Daguerre released the ladder with his left hand and swung backward to the side, his back crashing into the cabin door.

The flare whooshed by where his head had just been, plopping in the water with a hushed sizzle. Smoke trailed impotently from the water's surface.

Daguerre swung back onto the ladder and climbed the last few rungs. When he got to the top, Nasil was reaching into the open cabinet. Daguerre could see the small black box, no larger than an electric garage-door opener. He leaped forward, arms outstretched like a high diver going off a cliff.

His shoulder crashed into Nasil's chest and they both slammed into the metal railing around the flybridge. Together they sprawled to the floor, dazed. Nasil recovered first, rising slowly to his knees and firing off a roundhouse punch into Daguerre's jaw. Daguerre's head snapped to the right and bounced off the metal railing. He sagged dizzily.

Nasil was crawling toward the open cabinet now, hands reaching for the detonator. Daguerre clenched his teeth, twisted onto his right hip and kicked Nasil in the neck. The Centaur stumbled forward, his head cracking into the wheel, his hand accidentally shoving the gear lever.

Suddenly the engine whined at a high pitch and the boat began to strain against the ties. It rocked in the water as it attempted to pull free from the dock.

Daguerre sprang to his feet, but too late. Nasil held the detonator. He stood crouching on the flybridge, a triumphant smile on his lips as he clutched the black box to his chest. His breathing was labored and two of his front teeth were newly chipped. He coughed twice.

"If you press that," Daguerre said, "you'll be destroying six million dollars for your cause."

Nasil laughed, but it turned into a choke. "You people will never change. Money is easy to get in this world, my friend. What is important is that the hostages will die. That will fill the American people and their allies with fear and terror. Bend them just a little more our way. Make our logic a little easier to accept."

The boat began to pull even harder against the dock. The sounds of splintering wood echoed across the water.

"Then let me put it another way," Daguerre said. "If you press that I'll kill you."

Nasil laughed again, then looked deeper into Daguerre's eyes. The laughter stopped. He snarled once and held out the detonator, his finger moving toward the button.

"Hey, you men," someone from another boat farther down the dock shouted. "I don't care if you two get drunk and beat each other to hell and back. But goddamn it, you're pulling the whole goddamn dock with you."

When Nasil turned to look at the dock, Daguerre jumped forward and tried to grab the detonator. Nasil saw the movement and stepped backward. But he stepped back too far and flipped over the rail, grabbing desperately at Daguerre and pulling him over, too. They fell ten feet and landed in a tangle of crushed arms and bruised legs. Daguerre hit the deck with his wounded left arm and felt the nausea bubble into his throat.

The detonator had fallen out of Nasil's hand once they'd hit, and clattered to the back of the boat against the transom. Both men, still dazed from the fall, pulled themselves after it.

Nasil reached it first.

Daguerre was there a split second later, using what little strength he had left to swing a rocketing uppercut into Nasil's chin. Nasil sprawled backward, still holding the detonator. Daguerre reached for it.

But too late.

Nasil pressed the button and the explosion lit up the sky in a celebration of destruction. The *Sentry I* across the bay fired wood and metal scrap thirty feet into the air. Some of the flaming debris showered nearby boats, starting them on fire. There were horrified screams amid the orange crackling flames.

Daguerre looked over at the flaming *Sentry I*, searching the waters desperately for some sign of life. Had the woman managed to get them all overboard in time? He thought he saw some bobbing heads on the other side of the *Sentry I*, but he couldn't be sure. Might just be debris.

Daguerre stared at the calm smile of fulfillment on Nasil's face and felt his own body tightening, coiling with anger. The boat rocked furiously now and part of the dock had already torn away. Nasil's sweat- and blood-smeared face glistened in the light of the distant fires. His smug smile broadened. "We win," he said. "We always win."

At that moment, the rest of the dock ripped free and the boat lurched forward, throwing Daguerre off his feet. He managed to land on his right shoulder this time.

But Nasil was not so lucky. The boat's sudden thrust sent him somersaulting backward over the transom.

And into the churning propellers.

His horror-filled scream sliced the cool night as no scream had ever done before. Daguerre rushed forward. Nasil's hands gripped the lacquered wood of the transom, but the lower half of his body was caught in the grinding propellers. The sea boiled a bloody red foam around his waist.

His face was twisted in agony as he struggled to pull what was left of his ravaged body from the water. Daguerre reached out to grab Nasil's hands, but they were already slipping away, fingernails clawing across the lacquered wood.

Nasil screamed again, looked over his shoulder, saw his own sneakered foot float by. A sad look clenched his face. He let go of the boat.

Daguerre watched Nasil slide into the gnawing blades of the propellers, heard the strain as they struggled to shred such a large object. At last Nasil's face disappeared under the black water and for a moment Dagger thought he saw a fluorescent scar like a blazing comet glowing in the deep.

32

Daguerre looked over the edge of his *Los Angeles Times* and stared at the TV screen.

"And now a special report from correspondent Alexandra Knight."

"Turn it up!" a voice called from the bathroom.

Daguerre bounced off the bed and turned the volume up. "Don't you ever get tired of hearing this?"

Alex popped out of the bathroom, a towel around her hair and one around her body. "Hey, you're the big-shot hero who saved the day. Getting kissed and hugged on the dock by all those dripping wet women."

"Occupational hazard."

"All right, turn down the sound, but let's watch me."

Daguerre turned down the sound and they both sat on the edge of the bed and watched Alex give her on-camera report for the third time that day. When it was over, Alex jumped up from the bed and angrily shut the TV off. "They cut it this time!"

"Of course they cut it. This is a half-hour news show. The others were hour shows."

"Well, then let them cut something else. Hell, the president has been to China before. They could've cut that."

Daguerre laughed. "Look, you've already milked this one story for a new job, what else do you want?"

"It's only a local newscast. Not even a network affili-ate."

Daguerre smiled. "For now."

She smiled back and sat next to him. Her hands grazed his chest hairs as she kissed his left shoulder lightly and touched his bandage. "How's the arm?"

"Well, I don't think I'll be able to look a fish in the eye again without severe sympathy pains."

"And the head?" She kissed his forehead.

"Sore. I was never a good one for smiling through the pain. I'm a complainer."

She stood up. "Hmm, I'll bet." She took his face in both hands and stared into his eyes. "Answer some questions for me?"

"Oh, Christ. She gets a job with a Los Angeles TV sta-tion and already she wants an interview."

"No interview, Chris," she said seriously. "Just curiosity."

"Off the record?"

"Off the record."

"Okay."

She took a deep breath. "Why the incognito bit?"

"What do you mean?"

"You made me promise not to mention you in the story except as an 'informed source.' And I read your article. No mention of your name at all."

He shrugged.

"Come on, don't go all humble on me now. You told me the whole story. I *know* what you did."

"You made me tell you. It was the only way to keep you from broadcasting about me."

"Okay, okay. But you uncovered the smuggling ring in Mexico. By the way, Lieutenant Castillo is getting a lot of credit down there for that."

"He deserves it. Good man."

"All he'll tell the reporters is that he had an anonymous tip."

Daguerre flopped back on the bed and rooted through the paper for the sports section.

Alex knelt beside him. "And you managed to stall that maniac Nasil long enough so that all of the hostages got off the *Sentry I* before it exploded. If it hadn't been for you there would have been a lot worse than the few burns and broken bones that there were."

Daguerre said nothing.

"It's been a week now and still you won't talk about it. Even when we had dinner with your friends, Jimmy and Angie, you joked your way around all his questions. What's with you? You sick or something? Or just inhumanly noble?"

Daguerre smiled. "You know better."

"I thought so."

"All right, I'll explain it once then we'll drop it forever. Agreed?"

Alex nodded.

Daguerre frowned grimly. "Seven days ago the people of the world found out that Palestinian terrorists were smuggling themselves into the United States posing as illegal Mexican immigrants. They also found out that these terrorists had organized and almost succeeded at carrying out a kidnap-murder campaign unlike anything this country has ever seen. And what's happened since?"

"Well, there are investigations. The Senate and the FBI. The United Nations—"

"Right. Investigations. Do you want to know what will come of those 'investigations'?"

"What?"

"Zero. Zilch. *Nada*. Nothing. They will accuse the PLO, who will in turn denounce these actions as those of a fanatical splinter group. And it will all die down and disappear like your father's hairline."

"So you're saying what you did didn't make a difference?"

"Yes, it made a difference. To a lot of families right here in this city. And it'll make it a lot harder for terrorists to pull anything like this real soon. Here, anyway. But I can't get those awful words Nasil said out of my mind. 'We win. We always win.' I keep hearing that. I don't want that ever to be true."

"It won't," she said. "You won't let it happen. And I won't. Look at it this way, before there was just you fighting. Now there are two of us. Maybe by tomorrow there'll be more."

Daguerre chuckled. "You've convinced me."

"Good. Now can I turn the sound back up on the TV?"

"Sure. But why? Your segment is over."

"Her," Alex said, pointing at a young woman reporter interviewing the governor. "She's my competition."

Daguerre laughed loudly and grabbed Alex's wrist, pulling her back on the bed. Her towel fell open and she laughed, too.

"Alex," Daguerre said, "you have no competition."

The phone rang.

"No competition, huh?" Alex teased.

Daguerre nuzzled her neck while groping for the phone. "Yes?"

"Dagger, you bastard," the gruff voice barked. "We had a deal."

"No we didn't. You just thought we did."

"I gave you the information with the understanding you'd write the story for *me*. Not for the goddamn *Times*. I'd have paid you twice as much. More."

"Now you tell me."

Alex nibbled on his ear, bit it purposely hard.

"Oww."

"What's the matter?" Hannibal S. Kydd asked.

"Nothing." He playfully pushed Alex away with his foot. She giggled.

"Jesus, a woman, huh? I hope the poor twit has some idea what she's letting herself in for with a traitor like you."

"You want to tell her yourself?"

"Hell, no," Kydd said quickly, embarrassed. "Don't make me a part of whatever disgusting act you're commiting."

"She's a very nice woman. I think you'd like her."

"Not if she likes you," he snapped. He paused, his voice suddenly friendly. "Look, Dagger, why don't we just forget what's happened. Call it a misunderstanding, okay? Water under the bridge."

"You're making me nervous. What do you want?"

"Want? I want nothing. Whatever I want, I go out and take. It's just that I thought we made a pretty good team, you and me."

"A team?"

"Yeah, a team. Me digging up the background information; you out in the field. Hell of a team. So what if I didn't get the story, there are more important things in the world than a lousy story, right? At least we took a bite out of their pants on this one. Eh, Dagger? It may not end terrorism, but it's a start, damn it."

"Get to the point."

There was another pause. "It's just that I think we can do it again. I've got my sources for information. And with me feeding you, half your work is done. It would be your specialty, terrorism. I'd pay all your expenses and a bigger salary than you deserve, and you are my roving reporter. I've already set up a special hot line for you. Dial the number and you get straight to me, wherever I am. I'll send you whatever you need. You write the story any way you want. A free hand. How's that sound?"

"Forget it."

"Forget it?" the Captain blustered. "Why, goddamn it?"

"Because I don't trust you."

"We're not getting married, for chrissakes. We're doing something to make this a better world."

"When you start saying things like 'there are more important things in the world than a lousy story,' I start to worry."

"Don't you think there are more important things than a lousy story?"

"Yeah, but I don't think *you* think there are."

"You don't know me as well as you think, Dagger. Not nearly as well as you think. I have my reasons for doing this."

"Not interested."

"Think about it, at least. Call me back. That special number is—" He rattled the number off as Daguerre hung up.

"Who was that?" Alex said, snaking along Daguerre's naked body.

"Wrong number."

She perked up. "Another assignment?"

"Whoa, Alex. You've got your job, your assignments."

"Just testing," she smiled, pulling him on top of her, her hands sledding over the muscles of his back.

While he kissed her, Daguerre reached for the lamp switch next the bed, hesitated, walked his fingers along the tabletop. When he found the pen and pad he always kept handy, he jotted down the special number Hannibal S. Kydd had shouted into the phone.

Maybe later he'd call. Maybe. But not now. Not right now.

Readers everywhere thrill to Gold Eagle Books!

"I'm hooked. Your stories show the world as it really is. In my opinion, you put out some of the best damn books I've ever read."

—R.R., *Kokomo, IN

"I can't express in words how terrific your books are. I have read and reread them and I love them."

—D.M., Jacksonville, FL

"Your stories have a way of making people look deep inside at their own ideals and goals."

—H.W., Nashville, TN

"I can say without reservation that your fiction is the best I have ever read. I anxiously await more."

—R.R., Tujunga, CA

"I count myself lucky to find your titles once they hit the stands—the books sell like hotcakes."

—R.B., Redondo Beach, CA

"I feel that your adventures show a commitment and courage that so many are afraid to show."

—J.K., Rapid City, SD

*Names available on request